Elske Höweler

Left Behind

Orange House Publishing

ISBN: 978-1-7397197-0-8

Cover design by: Franziska Scheithauer

To Anna Elisabeth and Stijn

Chapter One

Amsterdam, February 1945

There was no light in the city. After dark, doors and windows had to be covered with heavy curtains, newspapers or whatever else came to hand. In truth, there wasn't a lot of light to black out. Most people only had dynamo torches, giving off the faintest of beams, to light their houses at night. Even those lucky enough to have something to burn, lit only the smallest of fires.

The streetlights hadn't been on for years. Going outside after blackout was too dangerous for most. Soldiers arrested anyone breaking curfew. And if you had the good fortune to avoid them, you'd still run the risk of getting lost or trying to go into the wrong house. Some doors had big white numbers painted on them to make them easier to recognise in the pitch black. The few people who had no choice but to go out after sunset walked close to the houses, touching them as they inched forward, guiding their way and keeping them as far as possible from the canals. They would follow the map they'd drawn up in their minds, trying at all times to spot familiar points along the way. But on a night as dark as this one, when even the moon wouldn't dare go out, everyone stayed in.

"Shush my poppet, time to go to sleep now. Mamma will be right here with you." Louise had just given Anna her midnight feed and was waiting for her to drift off to sleep safely in her cot so Louise too, could go back to bed.

Tap tap.

Even though the noise was faint, Louise jumped up out of her chair as soon as she heard it and, as if it was a natural reflex, blew out the candle. What was that noise and where was it coming from? She tilted her head, shut her eyes, and held her breath focusing completely on her hearing. She couldn't tell if the noise had come from the outside or in. Her heart rate increased, and her body stiffened.

Tap tap!

It sounded like it was coming from downstairs, like someone was tapping on the window. But who would do that in the middle of the night? Louise glanced over to the cot even though it was too dark to see anything. Her head snapped up as she heard the sound again. It was coming from the kitchen. There was someone at her back door. She felt her way out of the bedroom hoping the door wouldn't creak and wake Anna. Keeping close to the wall, she made her way across the landing and took hold of the banister. She stopped to listen but couldn't hear anything. If only Peter were here. He'd know what to do.

Peter! What if it was Peter? Maybe he'd escaped and made his way home. The fear evaporated, making way for a sense of excitement. Peter was home. Wishing she hadn't blown out the candle, Louise ran down the stairs as quickly as she dared in the dark. She rushed into the kitchen and ripped open the heavy curtain that blacked out the back door. What she saw made her freeze on the spot.

Chapter Two

Sarah came home early after cancelling her last two lessons. She didn't feel well. It felt like she had a boulder in her stomach, weighing her down and making it hard to move. At home she'd made a cup of chamomile tea and sat down with a magazine but couldn't focus on it. She felt weak and fatigued but unable to rest. Even her usual remedy, a hot bubble bath, didn't help. The feeling of unease remained.

Paul would be home soon. With heavy legs, she moved through the kitchen clearing up the mess he'd left from breakfast, muttering under her breath as to why he refused to tidy up after himself in the morning. As she wiped down the worktop, she heard the front door open.

The butterflies she used to feel when her husband came home had been replaced by a sadness that reminded her of when warm summer evenings made way for colder autumn nights.

"I'm in here," she called out. When he came into the kitchen, she walked towards him for a hug but Paul didn't notice and sat down at the table before they reached each other. Sarah's shoulders slumped and she changed course to get herself a glass of water instead.

"How was your day?" she asked him knowing she wouldn't get much of an answer. He looked tired and, like most evenings, he probably wasn't in the mood to talk.

"Okay, yours?"

"Not great." She told him about the odd feeling she'd had all day but he just nodded whilst looking at something on his phone. "I've put a pizza in the oven, I hope you don't mind, I didn't really feel like cooking.'

"That's fine." Paul got up to get a beer out of the fridge. "You want one?"

"No, thanks." Sarah hadn't had a beer in years. She found it kept her up at night so she stopped drinking it. She'd told him several times, yet he still offered.

As she was dishing up their dinner, the landline started ringing in the living room.

"I'll get it," she said, putting Paul's plate in front of him. Hers still stood on the worktop where it would remain untouched.

***

"Passports and tickets, please."

Sarah handed over the required documents.

"Have you been here on holiday?" asked the lady behind the counter. Sarah looked at her bright pink blusher, the mascara which had caused little clumps sticking to her lashes and the thick, black eyeliner and wondered how long it would take her to remove all that make-up in the evening.

"I live here," Sarah said with a friendly but fake smile, hoping she wouldn't be asked for more details. After nearly 15 years, she no longer enjoyed telling any random stranger the same story. Where it used to take her at least 10 minutes to cover every little romantic detail of the wonderful love story that had made her decide to leave everything behind and move to the UK, now she would just tell people she married a Brit and that was the end of it. It wasn't that she didn't want to talk about it, it was just that every time she told someone, they'd go on and on about how romantic it was and how lovely that they were still together. But, at the moment, it didn't feel like they were together and it certainly wasn't romantic anymore. Luckily, make-up lady wasn't interested in her passengers' life stories and Sarah couldn't blame her.

Despite the sad circumstances that made Sarah travel to Amsterdam, she still felt some of the same excitement she always did when she was on her way to Holland. Hearing her own language spoken by her fellow passengers and walking slightly more upright between the taller people from her home country made her smile. She stopped for a minute to look at the ferry through the terminal window. Standing next to her was a loved-up couple who were, in between kissing and giggling, taking selfies in front of the window with the ferry in the background. Sarah wondered if they actually wanted a photo to cherish the memory of their trip together, or just a snap to prove they were there, ready to be shared with their social media friends.

On the ferry, Sarah didn't follow the crowds of people, whose number only enhanced her loneliness, instead she went straight to her cabin. Alone and finally comfortable with letting her grief take control, she let her tears flow almost as fast as the raindrops racing down the window.

***

Sarah usually enjoyed the train journey from Hoek van Holland to Amsterdam. She loved watching the landscape which was so different to the one of her adopted country. The windmills, the endless flat fields separated by the little streams for the cows to drink out of and the many allotments running along the railway lines. But this time she didn't notice any of it. Every few seconds, she glanced at her phone lying on the little window sill style table. Still no word from Paul. She could really do with his support to get her through the next few days, even if it was from a distance. Arranging the funeral, making a start sorting through her mum's things and just being in her mum's house. She didn't want to do this on her own. She needed him. She knew he was busy at work and he couldn't just drop everything, but it hurt that he hadn't even tried to take some time off. No matter how big their problems were, surely he could help her through her mother's death. At least he'd said he'd try to come to the funeral. She checked her phone.

Again nothing.

It was nearly 7pm when Sarah walked out of Amsterdam Central Station looking for a taxi as she was too tired to drag her luggage onto a tram. Despite the rain, it was as busy as always. Herds of Asian tourists, seemingly unaware of the cliché image they produced as they snapped away on their cameras and then moved on quickly. Groups of youngsters, all on their phones, with backpacks so big they had to lean forward to keep their balance. In amongst the obvious tourists, the locals moved around smoothly, ignoring the throngs of visitors. The sea of bicycles parked outside the station made Sarah smile. She remembered the first time Paul came to Amsterdam with her. His amazement at the sheer number of bikes had only been topped by the fact that you could buy sausages from a vending machine. "Frikadellen, they're called," she'd told him laughing at the way he'd stared at the little compartment holding the long sausages. He'd eaten at least 10 of them in only a couple of days. She wasn't sure whether he really liked the taste of them or whether he just enjoyed putting in his euro in the slot and then opening the little door to release the snack from its warm cage. "Sausages on demand," he'd said as he tucked into another one, "I think I like Amsterdam."

It wasn't until Sarah got out of the taxi and was rummaging in her bag for the front door keys, that she felt a bit anxious about going in. Her mum had seemed fine when she'd last spoken to her a couple of days before, and, although she sounded tired and maybe even a bit distant, there'd been no sign of what was to happen two days later.

Chapter Three

Amsterdam, February 1945

Fear glimmered in the girl's eyes like balls of fire against the cloak of darkness. The shrubs lining the fence seemed to be making a steady and threatening approach. Down the bottom of the garden, the tall trees were swaying in the wind like angry giants stomping their feet. Nowhere looked safe. The girl's jaw was taut and her shoulders were hunched. Through the glass of the back door, Louise looked from the girl to the baby in her arms, she didn't look much older than her Anna. Her little lips were turning blue and she was quietly whimpering as if she knew the danger of making noise. In the distance, planes disturbed the quiet night with their deep foreboding rumble. No way of knowing if they were friends or enemies. Louise had to get them in quickly, before anyone saw them. Her shaking hands struggled with the lock. It had been stiff since last winter and Peter had promised countless times to fix it but never got around to it. Now the door was so rarely used, she had just left it. When it finally opened, Louise helped the girl inside. She struggled to walk in the shoes that were clearly far too big for her and she was wearing men's trousers but no coat. All she had to protect herself and her baby from the cold was a threadbare blanket.

Inside, Louise sat her down in the back room, grabbed her coat from the hallway and placed it gently on the girl's shoulders. Grateful for the little bit of warmth the coat offered, she wrapped it around herself and the baby. Louise took the piece of cloth from the water jug on the table and poured a glass. Every night before she went to bed, she filled up the jug and covered it with a cloth. There was no way of knowing whether there'd be running water in the morning or whether, like the gas, it'd be switched off overnight, without warning. This way, at least, she'd always have a jug full.

While the girl drank with quick little sips, Louise got her the bit of stale bread she was saving for her breakfast and swapped it for the now empty glass. She sat down next to the girl and watched her eat the bread, as if it was a sweet piece of chocolate cake.

"Better?" Louise asked, keeping her voice low and calm even though her heart and mind were racing. The girl nodded. She had black circles under her big brown eyes which didn't focus on any single point for longer than a second before quickly moving onto something else.

"Can you tell me your name?"

"Clara," she said with a hint of relief in her voice as if Louise knowing her name would somehow keep her safe. "And this is Camille."

"How old is she?" Louise asked, relieved to see some colour returning to the baby's lips.

"Three months," her voice not more than a whisper.

"Same as mine, Anna is asleep upstairs. My name is Louise." She thought she could see a flash of recognition in Clara's eyes as if she knew her name already. Louise wondered if the knock on her backdoor hadn't been the random choice she'd assumed it had been.

"Did you know to come here Clara? Did someone tell you to knock on my door?" Clara didn't answer but, from her trouser pocket, she took an envelope and put it on the table. Her eyes had grown even bigger and Louise regretted putting her on the spot. The envelope contained ration vouchers for the meagre weekly allowance for one adult. She put them away safely in the drawer with her own vouchers.

Louise looked at Camille and wondered whether Anna was the reason they had been sent to her. Hiding a baby was a lot easier with one already there. But who could have sent her? It must have been Peter as she didn't know anyone else in the resistance.

"Do you need any water for the baby? I don't have any milk."

"No, I feed her myself. She won't be a bother," Clara said as she moved Camille under her shirt to feed.

"I'm sure she won't, she looks a sweetheart." Louise smiled at Clara and through the fear she felt a spark of something else. A purpose.

When Camille finished feeding, Louise led them upstairs lighting the way with her dynamo torch. She pushed the lever down with her thumb to produce a short beam of faint light just enough for Clara to see where she was going. Every time Louise let the lever back up, and the stairs went dark again, Clara stopped for a second waiting for the next short burst of light. Louise showed Clara to her own bedroom. She gently

13

took Camille out of her arms and put her in the cot with Anna.

"They can keep each other warm. You can sleep in my bed tonight and I'll make you a place to stay tomorrow." For a second, she thought Clara would decline the offer of the bed but instead, she smiled and whispered a shaky "Thank you." Louise took her coat from Clara's shoulders and helped her in bed. She fell asleep as soon as her head laid down on the pillow.

Louise sat down on the chair next to Anna's cot, pulled her knees up so her feet were off the cold floor and covered herself with her coat. The tiredness she'd felt earlier had disappeared. In its place came a deep sense of dread. It wasn't hard to see why Clara had knocked on her door, the fear in her eyes told Louise everything she needed to know. What she didn't know was what to do next. Would she be brave enough to let them stay and risk her own life and that of Anna? Did she have any other choice?

**

In the attic, Louise could see her breath coming out of her mouth in clouds. The large dusty space would be home to Clara and Camille for as long as they needed it. It wouldn't be easy to sleep up there in the cold, but Louise would do whatever she could to make them as comfortable as possible. But first she had to make sure there was no risk of them being seen. Even though they wouldn't have a light up there, Louise had pinned a dark cloth over the only window. The makeshift bed she put in the middle of the space to keep them as far as possible away from any drafts, consisted of the cushions

14

of a chair she'd sawn into firewood earlier that winter and the only extra blanket that Louise had taken off her own bed. She had also gone through her wardrobe and taken one of her two knitted jumpers for Clara to wear, it was worn thin but it was the best she could do. For now, Anna and Camille would have to share what little baby clothes she had. Louise had already taken the last of Peter's jumpers out of the wardrobe to take apart and knit into baby clothes. It was his favourite and she was hoping to keep it for him for when he returned, but she knew he'd agree this was more important. A bucket in the corner would serve as a toilet and she brought up a few of Anna's nappies to keep them going for now. She'd have to look for an old towel to try and make some more or she'd never be able to keep up with washing them, let alone get them to dry in the cold weather. The final thing she did to make it a bit more bearable for Clara was taking up a couple of books for her to read during the day when there was a bit of light. She hadn't yet resorted to burning her books for warmth but it wouldn't be long before she had to. For Camille, she'd make a cuddly toy from some fabric scraps she had in her sewing box. There wasn't anything else she could do.

After their breakfast of watery potato peel soup, Louise suggested quietly that Clara and Camille should go up into the attic. She felt her cheeks heat up and was unable to look Clara in the eye. It felt wrong to send the two of them into such a cold hiding place but she didn't know what else to do. It was either that or send them on their way. The most difficult thing was that she couldn't ask anyone for help. It was impossible to know who to

15

trust. The only people she could rely on were her parents and she had no intention of dragging them into this. They had enough to worry about with mum's health not being so good recently. It'd be up to her alone to hide and feed her guests and also keep herself and Anna safe. Louise felt ashamed for briefly wishing she'd never opened the back door. Her life had seemed so hard before, but now, her new situation made the last few months look easy.

Clara wobbled on the stepladder leading up to the attic but she declined Louise's offer to take Camille.

'I need to know I can do this by myself, just in case I have to.' She was right, if there ever came a time, she'd have to get up those steps quickly, Louise might not be there to help her.

Chapter Four

The doctor who'd phoned Sarah with the news that she'd lost her last blood connection with this world, told her that her mum had been out shopping when she'd suffered a major stroke and collapsed. A bystander had called an ambulance and had sat with her until they arrived. Sarah was grateful she hadn't been alone but she couldn't escape the feeling of guilt that it should've been her holding her hand. She'd never know for sure how her mum felt about the absence of her only child in those last moments.

Help had arrived too late. Minutes after being admitted to hospital, and before the doctors had a chance to try and save her, she'd passed away. Sarah had been shocked when the doctor mentioned that the series of mini-strokes her mum had suffered over the last twelve months were probably the lead up to this big and final one. She was embarrassed to ask what he was talking about as her mum had never mentioned them. She was angry with her for hiding such a serious matter but thought her mum probably just didn't want to worry her.

Taking a deep breath, Sarah turned the key and opened the front door. She did a quick check of the living room, walked through the glass panelled sliding doors into the back room and poked her head into the kitchen. The house looked as if it had just been spring cleaned. Everything was tidy and in its place. Sarah smiled. No matter what, her mum always had her house in order.

"Always make sure your home is tidy and clean, Sarah. You never know who might drop by unannounced." She could still hear her say those words. It was one of the rules her mum lived by religiously. There were many more of them, she seemed to have one ready for any situation, and Sarah was half expecting to find a 'little book of Anna's rules' in her mum's desk.

When Sarah's mum married her dad, she moved in with him but only a few months after Sarah was born, tragedy had struck. Her father was killed in a car crash. Sarah's mum struggled with life as a new mum on her own in a town where she didn't really know anyone. After a few difficult months, she sold the house she shared, so briefly, with the love of her life and moved back to her childhood home where she lived for the rest of her life. It was a beautiful family home and had been in Sarah's family for almost 80 years. Her grandparents had bought it shortly after they got married, just before the second world war broke out and changed their lives forever. There was much more room than her mum could ever need. Sarah had asked a few years ago why she didn't sell it and buy something smaller in a quieter part of town. The house was probably worth a small fortune and the extra money would certainly have made life easier for her, but she wouldn't even consider it.

"I know it'd be the logical thing to do, Sarah," she'd say. "But I'm happy here. This is my home, this is where I was meant to be. I can't imagine ever living anywhere else." Even though selling made far more financial sense, Sarah agreed and was secretly pleased because she didn't want her mum to move either. She loved that house and everything about it. The location, far enough from the city centre to keep it tourist-free yet close enough so you could walk, the garden which was far bigger than most in Amsterdam, and the history. Her family had lived here for almost a century. But now she'd have to sell it. There was no family left to make it a home.

After taking her suitcases upstairs, Sarah went out in search of something to eat. She phoned Paul to let him know she'd arrived safely but he didn't answer. She told his voicemail all was well and she'd be in touch later.

***

'I'm home,' Paul said to the empty house. For a moment he stood on the door mat and listened to the silence, then he put his keys on the little table next to the front door and kicked off his shoes. With the post in his hand, he walked into the kitchen, took a beer out of the fridge, opened it, sat down and took a sip. His phone

19

rang but he didn't answer. He didn't even look to see who it was. They'd ring back if it was important. The sound of the beer sloshing in the bottle every time he took a sip and the humming of the fridge were the only sounds he could hear. He put his feet on the chair opposite, closed his eyes and enjoyed the stillness of the house.

The silence and the lack of human interaction relaxed Paul in a way that nothing else could. He wished there were more moments like this where he could do nothing but sit and have a beer. No need for people or conversation. Just himself and his silence. There were always people around him though and there was always so much noise. But now, here in his kitchen there was only him, a drink and the pain lurking around a dark corner in his heart. The pain, usually covered up by daily life, was beginning to expose itself even though Paul had no intention to let it out in the open where he knew it would swallow him up. Sarah accused him of not dealing with the pain. He knew she was right but he couldn't face it. It would rip him to pieces. Friends and colleagues had kindly told him he and Sarah were just dealing with it in different ways, but he knew that wasn't true. He wasn't dealing with it at all. He couldn't. It would kill him.

It was different for Sarah, she'd started grieving straight away. Nobody had expected her to get up in the morning to go to work or to even look after herself. But someone had to keep going. Somebody had to look after her. She'd been swallowed up by an ocean of grief and he was the only one who could keep her head above water. If he'd let her go, she would have drowned.

For weeks he'd rushed home in his lunch hour to make sure she'd eaten something and had a drink, then, after work, he would carry her to the bathroom and put her in the bath. At first, he washed her as you would a small child. She'd sit there and stare at the running water with tears streaming down her face, she didn't even seem to notice them. But, in time, she began to heal. She started washing herself and eventually she got out of bed to make a cup of tea, a snack, some lunch. Months went by before he came home and found her out of bed, cooking him dinner. He remembered feeling as if he'd ran across the finish line of a marathon. He'd done it, he'd fixed her. But who would fix him?

***

The pub where Sarah went for some dinner was called The Umbrella and was only a few minutes' walk from the house. It was a dark but cosy little place hidden in a narrow side street. It had red and white checked paper table cloths and slightly dirty glasses. But the wine was cheap and the food was much better than the decor suggested. It was also full of happy memories. Every summer, Sarah and her mum would eat there at least once. They enjoyed the friendly, laid back atmosphere. Sarah had the same as always, prawns in sweet chilli sauce with fried potatoes and salad. It didn't quite taste the same though, a different chef perhaps, or maybe it was the lack of company that made the food seem a little bland?

After dinner, Sarah went back to the house. She had a shower and found herself in her old bedroom. It hadn't changed much since she'd moved out to go to London for a year on a student exchange she'd been offered by the Royal Academy of Music. Little did she know she would meet the man of her dreams and move to Suffolk as soon as she'd finished her degree.

Sarah had often talked to her mum about re-decorating her old bedroom, but they never actually did. Neither wanted to let go of the happy memories they had from Sarah's childhood and even her slightly more challenging teenage years. Her wardrobe was still covered in Pearl Jam posters, and photos of her and her friends hung above her desk. Most of them featured Alice, her best friend since primary school. She was grateful for the familiarity of her teenage hideaway, but the room did not feel like home anymore, not without her mum.

Chapter Five

Amsterdam, February 1945

Louise and Clara sat as close to the wood-burning stove as possible. It was only 3pm and it was already getting dark. The small fire in the stove was never enough to heat up the whole of the back room. As soon as you stepped out of the little circle of heat it managed to produce, the cold took over. The gas fire in the front room hadn't been able to help Louise in her fight against the cold since the gas supply had been cut off. Like most people, she no longer attempted to heat up the whole house with the little fuel she had. The thick curtains hid the ice flowers on the windows and the door to the front room hadn't been opened since the first frost. There was no firewood left in the city and no transport to get any in. Trees were cut down in the middle of the night and many risked their lives stealing wood from wherever they could find it. A solid oak chair, however expensive it had once been, now meant enough fuel to make taste-less, but warm, potato peel soup for a week or two.

Louise had burnt most of the furniture she didn't desperately need. She had a few bits left which she was keeping just in case it got even colder. That morning, she'd been out in the garden to try and find anything she could burn but all she got was a few sticks and some leaves. Luckily, they were dry enough to start a small fire and she'd managed to make a hot, or at least reasonably warm, drink. They had run out of tea the week before and Louise hadn't been able to get any more but, at least, the hot water would warm Clara up a bit.

Clara couldn't stop shivering. Louise wondered if she'd be able to get her hands on some more blankets somehow. But where from? The whole city was cold. Nobody had enough clothes, blankets or wood to keep warm in this harshest of winters. And it didn't look like it was going to get warmer any time soon.

In front of the stove, on what used to be a coffee table, but that now only had half its legs and table top left, stood the little basket that she used as a cot down-stairs for Anna and now also Camille. The two of them were snuggled up under Anna's blanket. They seemed to comfort each other with their presence like twins. When Anna cried and Louise couldn't calm her down, she would put her next to Camille and the crying would stop. Louise looked at the two little babies who were so similar, but whose circumstances couldn't have been more different. Only because Camille was born Jewish and Anna was not.

"It must be tough not knowing where Daniel is," Louise said. Clara had been separated from her husband during the escape from their hiding place the year before.

"It is but I hold on to the hope that he's safe somewhere, like I am. What about Peter? Is he safe?"

The last Louise had heard of Peter's whereabouts was that he was imprisoned in Camp Amersfoort for working in the resistance movement. He'd been lucky though. The others that had been arrested with him were all killed shortly after their arrest, presumably because they had no skills that could be of any use to the Nazis. Peter was a highly respected and extremely intelligent chemistry professor, his knowledge was needed enough to keep him alive. However hard things were for her and Clara, she knew Peter had it much worse and she would keep strong for him. She had to.

Clara did whatever she could to help Louise. She often looked after Anna to give Louise time to do her daily chores and she never complained about anything, not even the cold. Louise couldn't imagine how cold it was up in the attic at night. Sometimes she had to defrost the contents of the bucket Clara used as a toilet before she could empty it and there wasn't a morning when Clara wasn't shivering as she gratefully accepted whatever Louise had managed to rustle up for breakfast.

"Thank you," she'd whisper through chattering teeth and blue lips. Often Louise would sit with her for a while holding Camille, sharing whatever little body warmth she had, whilst Clara took little sips of the hot water and slowly relaxed a bit as the warm liquid spread some heat through her body.

Despite the risk, every afternoon at about 3pm, Louise would knock on the attic hatch with the end of a broom stick she kept in her wardrobe. It was their signal that it was safe for Clara to come down. Clara would open the hatch and lower the wooden ladder. It wasn't easy climbing down with Camille in her arms and even worse when the cold made her shiver so much it was hard to hold on to the side of the ladder with one hand while her foot felt for the next step down. Louise worried about them being in that cold attic all day and she insisted they come down to warm themselves in front of the stove before settling down for another freezing night. She also wanted to keep some routine in Clara's life. She must be going mad in that attic all day with nothing to do and only a baby to talk to. If Louise thought her days were boring and time crept by like a sloth, Clara's must be so much worse. Sometimes, Louise got her hands on some tea or surrogate coffee but recently they'd had to make do with a cup of warm water. At first Clara had been nervous about putting their host in even more danger by being downstairs, but Louise wouldn't take no for an answer. They all needed this. Louise was very well aware of the risk she was taking and, even though she enjoyed her time with Clara, she was always on edge. Listening out for noises outside and never getting too comfortable. Just recently, a Jewish family who were in hiding around the corner were arrested because one of the children looked out of the window at the wrong time.

Still this hour of companionship gave them both so much she thought it was worth the risk. They always kept the hatch open and the stepladder in place so Clara could get back upstairs quickly if needed.

"You must be so proud of him," Clara said sipping her warm water. The small fire Louise had made to heat up a cup of water for them both had gone out and Louise pulled her cardigan tighter around her shoulders. She'd just told Clara about Peter's work for the resistance. She knew she shouldn't really talk about it, it wasn't safe to do so, but who was Clara going to tell?

"I am," Louise said. "I'm just not too sure he knows that. I didn't want him risking his life for the resistance anymore." Her cheeks coloured. "I was about to give birth and all I wanted was for us to be safe."

***

"You promised you'd stop." Louise said as she handed Peter his small bag with a change of clothes and the last slice of bread.

"How can I? How can I let other men fight on my behalf? I'm no coward." Louise hugged him as tight as she could manage with her ever growing belly.

"You're the bravest man I know, but right now your priority should be protecting your child. What would happen to us if you died?"

"Who says I'm going to die? Have I ever let you down before?"

Louise had to admit he hadn't. Peter gently released her hands from behind his back and kissed her. "I have to go. They'll be waiting."

"When will you be back?"

"Soon, I hope. Soon. Stay safe my love," he said and disappeared into the dark night.

Chapter Six

Sarah loved shopping in Holland. It was like stepping into a time machine and travelling all the way through her life. The sweets she wanted as a child but she never got. The cheap wine she drunk with Alice before the "alcohol-free" school dance. And the treats she now enjoyed so much because she couldn't get them in England. Her eyes cast over all the different bags of liquorice, sweet, salty or extra salty, and she dropped a couple in her basket. Shame it wasn't December, otherwise she could have stocked up on pepernoten, the little spiced biscuits the size of a penny that were one of the traditional treats for the St Nicholas celebrations on the fifth of December. And cheese. Fresh Dutch cheese. Not the plastic wrapped sweaty Gouda you can now get in Tesco but cut from the wheel right in front of you after being offered a slice to taste.

Back at the house she put the shopping away wondering what to eat first. The TO DO list she'd made the night before was staring at her from the fridge. Her shopping trip was partly because she needed food but it also doubled as quite an effective delay tactic. Every item on the list of chores required her to say out loud those words she wished weren't true. My mother has passed away. My mum is dead. Saying it in different ways did not change the meaning or the extensive impact on Sarah's life. She had an hour until her appointment with the funeral director and she needed to keep busy. The temptation to sit down and wallow in her grief was strong but she knew how dangerous it was to let her thoughts roam free. Better to try and get through the day without thinking too much. Thinking would only lead to remembering the last time she arranged a funeral. The little purple dress they'd chosen so carefully. And that tiny coffin. That teeny tiny coffin being lowered into that massive looking grave was an image Sarah would never be able to wipe from her memory. She could feel the images pushing their way to the front of her mind, threatening to clear the mental wall she'd built to keep them at a distance. She couldn't let them back in. They'd draw her back to that dark place that Paul had only just managed to drag her out of. If she'd let herself go there now, she'd never come back out. She needed to focus and for that she needed a caffeine boost. She started a pot of cinnamon coffee - her favourite - and made toast with hagelslag. Hot buttery toast with chocolate sprinkles that would literally melt in the mouth. Paul never understood how she could enjoy sweet toast like that, especially first thing in the morning. But then there were a lot of things Paul didn't understand.

After a few minutes the coffee machine started to make the funny gurgling noises Sarah was so fond of. It was one of those old-fashioned machines that made proper coffee, none of the creamy stuff you get from the modern machines that Paul insisted on. Just proper, strong, black coffee. The way Sarah thought it was meant to be. She poured herself a big mug and inhaled the slightly bitter aroma with a sweet hint of cinnamon. Perfect. She loved nothing more than a good cup of coffee and having this big steaming mug on her mum's desk made the tasks ahead seem that little bit less daunting.

Surprisingly, she'd made it through the morning without crying. The gentleman from the funeral directors was a lot younger than Sarah had expected. She smiled at her own naive assumption that everyone working in his profession would be old and wearing stiff suits and ties. The young man's friendly, yet professional, manner made her feel at ease. A few times she struggled to keep her tears back, especially when choosing the coffin, but overall it didn't go too bad. It only took a couple of hours to sort everything out. The obituary that would go in tomorrow's paper, the cards that'd be sent to Anna's friends and the flowers to go on the coffin. The service would be held on Wednesday morning at 10 and there was plenty of time for Sarah to think of what music she'd want played and what readings she'd like. It seemed strange that something as final as a funeral was so quick and relatively easy to arrange. However, the effort of talking to people without bursting into tears had drained her of all energy. She had nothing left and sat down on the sofa with another comforting mug of coffee reminiscing about the countless times she'd sat in that same spot telling her mum all about whatever was troubling her at the time. No matter what she was facing, it never took long for the problems, that seemed the end of the world to start with, to reduce back down to their actual size and importance again. And with a little guidance from her mum, she'd soon feel strong enough to deal with anything life would throw at her. But sitting there, on her own, no comfort came. There were no soothing words or calming cups of tea. The blind faith there would always be someone there to make things better was gone.

Sarah's mind was full of memories, regrets and guilt for not being with her mum when she passed away. She knew her mum had made her peace with Sarah living in England and had always enjoyed coming to visit her. She loved discovering new places and meeting new people. It was only a few months since she'd last visited, for the last time it turned out. During one of their walks along the Suffolk coast Sarah had expressed her concern for not being there for her mum if she ever need help. Sarah was told not to worry, she had plenty of friends who could help her if she needed it. 'I do have a life you know, I don't just sit on the sofa waiting for you to ring!' She'd joked when Sarah wouldn't leave the subject be. She knew that her mum was more than capable of looking after herself and her worries stemmed more from her own feeling of guilt, than actual concern about her mother's wellbeing. It was the last time the subject was discussed. Would things have been different if Sarah hadn't moved to England? Probably not. But she couldn't help blaming herself for not being there when her mum needed her most.

Directly opposite the sofa, where most people would have their tv, was her mum's most beloved possession. A ceiling high, wall-to-wall bookcase filled to the brim with books in many genres. Historical novels, literary fiction, classics, mysteries and the odd thriller. As a little girl, Sarah used to love playing with books. And even though they were very precious, as long as she was careful, she was always allowed to use them as part of her games. She'd spend hours playing library, bookshop or use them as bricks to build a fort. There were times when Sarah desperately wanted to have a brother or a sister to play with. Most of her friends from school had siblings and even though they always told her how lucky she was not having to put up with a little brother or sister, she couldn't help but feel a bit jealous. Even though she had a very happy childhood, her mum would always play with her, the wish for a sibling ran deep. Someone bound to her by blood ties, someone who would always be there because they were family. She always thought, one day, she'd have her own family. She wanted two, three or maybe even four kids, so they'd never be alone.

Sarah walked from one end of the bookcase to the other running her fingers along the spines of the books that lived on the favourite shelf. The one in the middle that your eyes were first drawn to when you sat on the sofa. It housed only the best and most special books of all. The ones that would be read again and again. Many of Sarah and her mum's phone conversations started with 'What are you reading?' And her mum would tell her all about the book she was devouring at the time. After her music, reading was Sarah's biggest passion.

The way a story could whisk you away to another world, let you become a different person and live someone else's life had become more and more appealing over the last few years. Stories were her way of coping.

Halfway down the favourite shelf, she stopped. In between Love in the Time of Cholera by Gabriel Garcia Márquez and Carlos Ruiz Zafón's The Shadow of the Wind was a little wooden box standing on its side. Sarah couldn't remember seeing it there before, yet somehow it looked familiar. She tried to think back if anything other than books had ever sat on that shelf but she was pretty sure nothing ever had. The favourite shelf was a crowded place and when a new novel was deemed good enough to take this pride of place, which very rarely happened, books were carefully re-arranged and time was taken to decide which old favourite would have to be demoted to a different, less special, shelf. No, it had definitely not been there before. But why was it there now? And what was in it? Standing up, it looked just like an old book with a worn spine. The box was made of a light coloured wood, oak maybe, and just a little bigger than the books surrounding it. A swirly pattern was carved in the wood along the sides and on the lid was a painted scene of a woman staring out at sea holding her hand above her eyes to protect them from the sun. Her white skirt billowed in the wind. It was a pretty but somehow sad picture, like the woman was looking out for something that, she knew, would not come.

Sarah sat on the sofa with the wooden box on her lap. Her fingers running along the carved edges with a sense of ease. As if her fingers remembered feeling it before. It reminded her of being a little girl, in the same way that the smell of sun cream instantly reminds you of summer holiday. Why did it feel so familiar when she was sure she'd never seen it before? Or maybe she had? She looked at the image and wondered if it was maybe a painting that she'd seen in a museum or online somewhere. She couldn't remember. She wanted to open it but hesitated. It felt important, as if after opening it nothing would ever be the same again. Too curious to resist any longer, she opened the box.

Chapter Seven

Fear was the only thing that broke the monotony of war. Fear of the bombs, the cold, even fear of hunger. It surely was a distraction from the repetitive daily routine, but not a welcome one. In the early days of occupation Louise had often wondered what life would be like as the war went on. She imagined lots of scenarios, but what she'd never expected was the boredom. Every day was pretty much the same as the last. Queueing up for food, trying to find firewood, thinking of how to make the potato peel soup taste slightly better without any ingredients. Struggling to wash all the nappies without soap and then, even worse, getting them dry in a cold and damp house.

The curfew and the compulsory black-out made for seemingly endless evenings. Owning a wireless had become illegal two years ago and, without electricity, light had become a scarce commodity. She'd tried reading by the light of her dynamo torch but had given up after a few pages as her thumb cramped up with pain from continuously pushing the lever up and down. She only had half a candle left which she kept for feeding Anna in the night, she couldn't waste it on reading. There was not much else to do than go to bed as soon as Anna had fallen asleep. With the one benefit that, at least, in bed she was reasonably warm.

The only break from her normal routine was her weekly visit to her parents. She used to go at least twice or sometimes even three times a week, especially since Peter had been on the run, but that was when she could still hop on a tram. Now, as there was no public transport anymore, she only braved the hour long walk to go and see them on Saturday mornings. It was the highlight of her week. No matter how miserable the times, or how limited the rations, Saturday lunch was always a bit of a feast compared to what she ate the rest of the week. Louise had no idea how her mother managed it, but even if the only ingredients available were tulip bulbs and potato peel, the food always tasted good.

Louise's neighbours knew about her weekly visit, which meant that Clara had to keep Camille quiet for as long as Louise was out. Any noise coming from her house, could raise suspicion and put all their lives at risk. Even though Louise skipped having breakfast to give Clara her share, she couldn't look Clara in the eye when she brought her food up that morning. All she had to offer for the cold long day ahead was half a slice of bread, a cup of weak broth and a jug of water. Clara had warmed her hands on the cup smiling as if she'd been given a present she had always wanted.

"I'll come back a bit earlier today," Louise said.

"No, don't. Do exactly the same as always. If someone notices you coming back early, they might start asking questions." Louise hadn't thought of that and she felt embarrassed for her naivety. How could she possibly keep them safe?

"Don't worry about us, we'll be fine."

Louise hesitated.

"You'd better go, you don't want to be late for lunch," Clara said with a wink.

Louise made her way down the stepladder wondering how Clara still managed to keep her sense of humour in the darkest hours of her life. As she was getting Anna ready to go, she realised she had no idea whether Clara knew if her parents were still alive. Thinking about it, she didn't know much about Clara's life at all. She'd ask her later today.

The streets looked strangely empty on Saturday mornings, more like a ghost town than a capital city. With the shops and soup kitchens shut there were no queues of people trying to get their hands on whatever food was available. The only people outside were the ones who had somewhere to go. Anyone else stayed in the safety of their homes, protected from the worst of the weather. But no matter how cold, wet or windy it was, there were always soldiers about. As if they were worried they'd miss an opportunity to arrest someone, or even just to bully them for their own amusement.

Whenever Louise saw one, or even worse a group of them, standing on the pavement smoking their cigarettes, she would turn into a side street as soon as she could. Even if that meant walking in the cold or icy rain for much longer. When she didn't have a choice but to keep walking, she would speed up and keep her eyes focused firmly on Anna, praying she could pass unnoticed.

Today, there seemed to be more soldiers around than normal. They were on every corner, at every crossing, making it impossible to avoid them. Despite her fear, Louise was curious as to why there were so many of them. Was there something going on? Just ahead of her, a group of them stopped an old lady to ask for her identity card. She gave it to them and her big eyes scanned their harsh faces. Louise stopped and looked for a different route. There was another group of them on the other side of the road stopping people to ask them for their papers. A truck was parked half on the pavement and she could see some men sitting inside. They had their heads down and a gun pointed at them by a soldier who looked like he should still be in school. Despite the cold, Louise was sweating. Maybe she should turn around. But before she could manoeuvre the pram in the opposite direction, one of the soldiers noticed her and marched towards her. She couldn't walk away now. Keeping her eyes down, she heard his heavy boots come closer. The stomping sound of the marching on the pavement, harsh and terrifying, filled Louise's head until it stopped suddenly.

"Identity Card!" he barked at her.

She rummaged through her bag. Where was it? Had she forgotten it? She felt the impatience of the soldier.

Sweat tickled her neck. Would they arrest her if she didn't have it? Then who'd look after Clara and Camille? Finally, she found it and held it out without looking up. The soldier took it off her and studied it. He didn't give it back.

"Where are you going?"

"To see my parents. I go every Saturday," Louise said, still not looking up.

"Take the baby out," the soldier said much louder than necessary whilst waving his gun at Anna. Louise quickly grabbed her and held her as close to her chest as she could, whispering soothing words into her tiny ear. She'd woken up and started whimpering. "Don't cry, poppet, everything will be fine," she whispered not at all confident that it would. The soldier was ripping the blankets out of the pram and throwing them on the wet pavement. The last thing Louise saw landing in a puddle was Anna's cuddly bunny that she had knitted for her with the wool from a pair of Peter's gloves. She didn't dare pick it up and looked at it soaking up the cold mud. The soldier hit the bottom of the pram so hard with the butt of his gun that Louise worried it would break. Not having found whatever he was looking for, the soldier shoved her identity card back at her and told her to go. He spun around on his heels and made his way back to his fellow tormentors. He didn't notice he stepped on the bunny. With one hand Louise gathered the filthy bedding and the cuddly toy and put it back in the pram. She turned around and walked back the way she came as fast as she could with Anna on her shoulder and pushing the pram with one hand.

When she finally made it to her parent's house, after taking a couple of detours to avoid even more soldiers, she was over an hour late. If the curtains hadn't been closed to keep as much of the warmth in as possible, her mother surely would have been sitting at the window looking out for her. It took only a couple of seconds after she knocked before the door opened and her mother rushed her inside. Louise's dad, Jan, followed close behind to get the pram inside. Having, at last, made it to the safe space of her childhood home, Louise couldn't hold her tears back any longer. Her mother, Greta, took Anna out of her daughter's freezing hands and Jan helped Louise into the chair nearest the stove. She let her tears flow and her parents waited patiently until she was ready to tell them what happened.

"Luckily Anna didn't start screaming. I dread to think what that soldier would have done to her or me," Louise concluded her account of this morning's walk.

"You really shouldn't be walking all this way on your own Lou. It's too dangerous," her father said.

"I can't just stop coming to see you, Pappa, it wouldn't be right. And it's the best day of my week, I'd be miserable if I'd have to miss this as well. It's bad enough on my own all week." Louise felt her cheeks flush in shame because of the lie but there was no other way. She couldn't tell them about Clara, they were worried enough as it were. Jan put his arm around her shoulder and gave it a squeeze. Louise leaned into him and for a moment she felt like a little girl again, not a woman risking her life by hiding Jews in her attic.

"Let's sit down for lunch. You must be starving, my love," Greta said as she lifted up the lid of the pot bubbling on the stove.

"Sorry for being late Mamma, I didn't mean to make you wait."

"Don't be silly, darling. It's hardly your fault. And your father took hours to get the stove going this morning so lunch would have been late anyway." Greta winked at Louise who let slip a little smile.

"It's because we only have wet sticks to burn," her father complained. "Nobody can make a fire with that."

"You should count yourself lucky we have anything to burn at all, my dear. There are plenty of people who have already burned their furniture and all they have left now to get their stove going are a few books, and they certainly won't last them until the end of winter."

Using furniture for firewood had become pretty common these days. Quite a few times when Louise visited over the last couple of months, she'd noticed the marks in the carpet where an item of furniture once stood. And when she saw the stove burning so fiercely, she realised why her mother had put her coat on the stairs. Louise's own coat rack had given her enough wood to cook dinner for a week but it looked like her parents hadn't been as economical with theirs. She hadn't been in a room this warm for a long time. She felt uncomfortable knowing that her parents were burning their furniture just so the house would be warm and lunch would be cooked for when she came around, but she knew it would be no use saying anything about it. Her parents had always put her first and no enemy in the world would change that.

Lunch consisted of an onion and potato stew and the nicest bread she had eaten in ages. She suspected a large chunk of lifesavings were spent on the black market and that her parents had gone hungry for a while, saving their own rations, to make this meal possible.

"This is another reason I will take the risk walking here," Louise said pointing her spoon at her plate. "Your food always tastes so much better than anything that I manage to make." Before her father could make a move to help himself to a bit more Greta took the pan off the table.

"You can take the rest home with you, my dear."

"Thank you, mamma, Clara would love this."

Heat rose to Louise's cheeks and her spoon dropped on her plate with a clatter. They all stopped what they were doing and looked at each other with frightened eyes. Everything was still, as if time was as frozen as the ground outside. Only Anna, who was dozing in her pram in front of the fire, continued to breathe. Louise didn't know what to say or do. Should she make up a friend called Clara who was struggling? She desperately wanted to tell them the truth but she knew she couldn't. Jan looked at his daughter with what looked like a hint of pride in his eyes. Did they already know? But how could they? She hadn't told a soul. Jan took Louise's hand and squeezed it tight. Greta cleared her throat and, as if nothing had happened, took the plates to the kitchen and rinsed them although there was nothing left on the plates to wash off. Louise had missed the opportunity to explain away what she'd said and she sat in silence, holding her father's hand, until her mother returned with a tiny package.

"I have a real treat for you, Louise. I managed to get my hands on some coffee. Proper coffee." Greta looked pleased with herself, Louise guessed she'd have been looking forward to this moment all day.

"How much did that cost you, mamma?" Louise asked looking at the package with such longing she could almost taste the hot black liquid already. Greta waved the question away and gave Louise the coffee and a kiss on the top of her head.

"Aren't we going to have it now?" Jan asked. Louise knew her father missed his beloved daily cup of coffee even more desperately than she did and she wouldn't want him to miss the chance to have a cup. Besides, the only way you could get coffee these days was by spending a fortune on the black market, so it was only fair they shared it.

"Will you make it please, mamma?"

"Of course, my dear, if that's what you want."

The coffee was weak but to Louise it tasted strong and bitter in the lovely way that only coffee could. They drank it in silence savouring every sip. Louise inhaled the satisfying aroma and smiled when she looked at her father. He was drinking with his eyes closed. Greta looked pleased that her efforts were rewarded with this little moment of bliss. For a few minutes they were all able to forget about the horrific things happening in the outside world. When the coffee was gone, silence remained until Anna, with a loud wail, made it clear she was hungry.

"I'd better head back soon," Louise said after feeding Anna, making no real move to leave.

When she'd met Peter she couldn't wait to marry him and get a place for just the two of them. She loved her parents dearly but to run her own household and to be alone with Peter was like a dream. Now, with Peter gone, she wanted nothing more than for her mother to look after her, even if only for a few days. Of course, that wasn't possible. Who would feed Clara if she didn't go home? Slowly, she dragged herself up from the chair and started wrapping up as warm as she could.

"I've washed Anna's blankets and bunny for you. They're not dry yet but I have a spare blanket for you to wrap her in." Louise doubted the blanket was 'spare' but she was grateful to have it so she didn't have to carry her all the way home. Her arms still ached from holding her most of the way there.

"I've also packed a couple of towels we don't really need. I thought you could make them into spare nappies for Anna or something." Louise tried to read the look her mother gave her but she couldn't decipher it.

"Thank you, mamma. I'll bring the blanket back next Saturday."

"Don't worry about that love, you need it more than we do. Jan, get the vouchers for me, please?"

Her father got up, rummaged in the cupboard behind him and handed Louise an envelope.

"There's some extra food vouchers in there for you."

"Where did you get those?" Louise whispered.

"Don't ask, Louise," her father answered. "And don't use them in your usual place, spread them out as much as you can." Louise gave her father a tight hug.

"Thanks, pappa."

Greta held her daughter for a long time as they said goodbye at the door.

"Look after yourself, love. And be careful."

Chapter Eight

Inside the box was a square notebook covered in flowery fabric that had worn thin at the corners and lost the bright colours Sarah suspected it once had. She took it out of the box handling it with the same care as you would a valuable piece of antique jewellery. She turned it over in her hands a few times. Should she open it? She wanted to know what it was but also felt uncomfortable about finding out. It felt so strange going through her mum's personal belongings, like she was spying on her. What if it was her mum's diary? Sarah wasn't sure if she wanted to read that. And more importantly, would her mum want her to? Unsure of what to do, Sarah stared at the empty space in the bookcase where the box had been earlier.

If her mum didn't want her to read it, why would she have left it there, in such an obvious place, wedged in between Sarah's two favourite books? In fact, it looked more like it had been left there on purpose. Right in the middle of her bookcase, just waiting to be found. The more she thought about it the more she convinced herself that she was meant to find it. Trying to ignore the uncomfortable feeling of invading her mum's privacy, Sarah carefully turned to the first page and started reading.

Her coffee had gone cold long before she looked up from the scribbly writing. It took her a while to come back to reality. The notebook was indeed a diary, but not her mum's. It was her nanna's. She'd written it during the winter of 1945, the last few months of the Second World War that later became known as the Hunger Winter.

Sarah knew very little about her nanna's past. Neither her mum nor her nanna had spoken about it much, and the war was a subject that was carefully avoided. The only thing Sarah knew was that her granddad and both her great-grandparents had died during the war, although she didn't know the circumstances. She'd asked several times but her nanna had never been forthcoming with any information, no stories were told and no experiences shared. When Sarah was in year 6 at primary school, they did a project on the war and they were all sent home with the assignment to find out what their grandparents did between 1940 and 1945. She'd been excited to finally find out more. Surely they'd tell her something now she needed it for school. But they didn't. Her nanna had flat out refused to talk to her about it. Sarah had been very upset. Not only because she'd fail the assignment but even more so because she felt let down by the two people she loved most in the world and she had no idea why.

"Why doesn't Nanna want me to know?" She'd asked her mum. "I'm old enough to deal with it. I know the things that happened, they told us in school."

"It's not that she doesn't want you to know, sweetheart. It was a tough time for her and talking about it will bring it all back. We shouldn't force her to re-live those horrific experiences."

"Then why don't you tell me?" Her mum had given her a kiss on her forehead.

"It's not my story to tell, my darling."

That evening, Sarah made up a story for her assignment in which her grandad died from pneumonia while her nanna worked as a nurse in a local hospital up until her mum was born. She managed to pass the assignment but never asked about the past again.

Sarah shut the diary and exhaled a breath she'd held for a long time. She rubbed her eyes. Her mind felt like it was chasing itself, like a dog running after its own tail. She was shocked by what she'd read in the first few pages. It had become clear straight away that her nanna had had a lot more to deal with than just the hunger, the cold and the fear of bombers; as if that wasn't enough. Her husband, Sarah's grandfather, whose cause of death Sarah never knew, worked for the resistance movement and had been arrested by the Nazis and was held in Camp Amersfoort. Her nanna lived in constant fear of his life. What surprised Sarah even more was reading about Clara and Camille, a young Jewish woman and her baby who had been forced to move from their last hiding place for fear of being betrayed, and who her

47

nanna hid in the attic. That same attic that now belonged to her.

Sarah put the diary back in its box, unable to take in any more. After so many years of not knowing anything about such an important time in her family's history, she now had the personal account of her nanna. Her own flesh and blood. To finally have a look into her family's past like this was the most precious gift her mum could have given her. But why did she not give it to her before? Why wait so long? Why wait until anyone who could answer her questions was dead? Regardless of the reasons for waiting, Sarah was grateful she finally knew more. She remembered how her mum had often told her about how incredibly strong and brave her nanna was. She'd never doubted this, but it was only now beginning to dawn on her what her mum had really meant. It was impossible to grasp how hard those years of war must have been for a young mother on her own. And Sarah started to understand why it might have been so difficult for her to talk about it.

"Are you here yet? Do you need drinks?"

A message from Alice. Sarah had meant to text her this morning but it had slipped her mind. She'd known Alice since her first day of primary school when Alice shared her biscuit with her at snack time. They had been best friends ever since and she couldn't wait to catch up with her.

"Yes, and YES!"

"Good, good. In or out?"

Sarah smiled. They had never needed many words to communicate. Often all it took was a certain look or a little nod. It used to frustrate Paul because he always felt very much on the side-lines, which, when it came to Sarah and Alice, he was. And so was everyone else.

"In please"

"Okay, see you at 8. I'll bring wine"

Sarah felt a lot better knowing after such a difficult day she'd have a "girlie night in" to look forward to. She still hadn't heard from Paul despite texting him several times and she needed some moral support. A catch up with her oldest friend was just what she needed.

Before she could relax though, she had to tackle choosing her mum's funeral outfit. Sarah wanted to do her proud and give her the send off she deserved in the clothes that she loved, so she put the box with the diary back where she found it and dragged her unwilling feet upstairs to her mum's room.

She opened the wardrobe and flopped onto the bed looking at the neat row of outfits. Memories of the occasions when they were worn started flooding her brain and her eyes, blurring the sea of pastels in front of her. As a teenager she'd often been frustrated by the light colours that her mum always dressed in while she herself craved deep purple, dark green and the blackest of black to match her teenage moods. But in her mum's wardrobe there wasn't a single black garment to be seen. Only light and bright was allowed. As Sarah grew up she ditched some of the dark colours she shrouded herself in during high school and started to appreciate her mum's style. She grew to love how she, regardless of what was fashionable or deemed appropriate, wouldn't change her wardrobe for anyone.

The outfit she had worn to Sarah and Paul's wedding still took pride of place. They had chosen it together during one of Sarah's summer visits. They'd spent hours going from one shop to the next not finding anything Anna approved of. Nothing was special enough. After lunch and a glass of wine Sarah asked where she wanted to go next.

"Let's go to the posh end of town." Anna said with a smile on her face.

They linked arms and giggled into the first designer boutique they saw. Whilst her mum explained to one of the shop assistants what she wanted or, mostly, what she didn't want, Sarah was offered a seat and a glass of champagne.

"I could get used to this," she whispered as the shop assistant walked around the shop looking for outfits that matched the requirements. In true Anna style, everything with even a hint of dark colour was dismissed straight away.

"If you don't like dark colours, you should try this," said the assistant who'd given Sarah her champagne. She pointed at a floaty, cream coloured trouser combination. Anna frowned at it but took it anyway to try on. When she came out of the changing room looking a bride herself, Sarah applauded in excitement. It fitted as if it had been tailor-made and Sarah knew it would look perfect next to her own dress which was a deep red.

"I'll take it," Anna said without a hint of doubt in her voice. On the big day she looked beautiful and her eyes glinted with pride as she waltzed around the room like a queen attending her princess's wedding. Sarah remembered feeling so lucky to have her there.

"Oh mum, I feel so alone," Sarah said to the open wardrobe. She'd had some very tough times the last few years, but knowing her mum was on the other end of a phone, always kept her going. She wondered if this was how her mum felt when Sarah's dad died all those years ago. She had no memories of him, just a photo album that only featured him in the first half and the stories her mum had told her about him. When she was about nine years old, she asked her mum if she would ever marry again.

"I was going to be with your dad forever. He was my soulmate. How could anyone ever take his place?" She answered.

"But aren't you ever lonely?"

"How can I be lonely when I have you?"

Even at this young age Sarah knew this probably wasn't true, but she was happy to at least pretend to believe it. In a way she liked not having to share her mum with anyone. It had always been her and her mum. But now it was just her. No back-up. Nothing to look forward to. If Emma hadn't died, she'd still have something to keep her going. Losing your mum was, although incredibly sad, the natural order of things and if she had her daughter to live for, it would have been different. If Emma would still make her smile every morning, she'd be happy again. Eventually.

***

"She'd have loved the outfit," Alice said when Sarah showed her the light green trouser suit with the white blouse and pearl earrings she'd chosen. It'd taken her hours to try and work out what her mum would have wanted but, in the end, Sarah decided on what she loved seeing her mum wear most. "Classic and bright. She always looked so pretty in pastels."

Sarah smiled, that was exactly what she thought.

"I remember when she showed me what she wore to my dad's funeral," Sarah said with a giggle. "It was a baby pink mini dress with little white kitten heels. As you can imagine, it was not well received, but it was my dad's favourite and that was all that mattered to her."

"She rocked that mum of yours."

"She did, she really did."

Sarah picked up her glass of perfectly cooled Sauvignon Blanc and let the wine guide the grief back down her throat.

"Do you know what you're wearing to the funeral?"

"Not really. Nothing I've brought with me seems right."

"You should go shopping tomorrow, get yourself something nice. Your mum would've wanted that. You can always put it on your credit card and let Paul worry about paying it off." Sarah looked at her best friend knowing exactly what was coming next.

"I take it he is too busy to support his grieving wife?"

"Something like that." Sarah leaned over to get the bottle of wine. "If we're going to talk about Paul, we need more of this." Alice downed her wine and held out her glass.

"Finally, he's good for something."

Sarah knew Paul's shortcomings were many, but she didn't like anyone badmouthing him and she threw Alice a look that said as much. Alice only tolerated Paul for Sarah's sake and hoped he'd prove her wrong and turn out to be a half decent husband who made her friend at least a little happy. Now she worried she'd been right all along and that maybe she should've done more to make Sarah see she deserved better than what Paul offered. She deserved the best and, just as Alice had feared, in the end, Paul wasn't it. Sarah, however, still tried to hold on to the man he used to be when she fell in love with him and hoped that, one day, things would go back to the way they were before and they'd live happily ever after.

"Do you want the short version or the long?" Sarah asked. Alice let a puff of breath escape from her mouth.

"The long, of course."

Sarah filled Alice in on how things had deteriorated even further since they'd last spoken. How they'd been so distant that Sarah had no idea how to even start bridging the gap between them that was widening by the day.

"It's like we're roommates. We have dinner together, some nights at least, watch some TV and go to bed. We don't talk, we don't go out and I can't remember the last time we had sex."

"Then why are you still with him?"

"Because I love him."

"Do you?" The question hung in the air like a thunderstorm lurking in the distance.

"I think he blames me for her death," Sarah whispered.

"Really? Why would he?" Sarah shrugged and shook her head.

"I don't know."

"Nonsense. You did everything you could. And it wasn't like he was there to help, was he?" Alice was right. By the time Paul had come home from work, after ignoring several pleas from Sarah, they'd already left for the hospital. Sarah tried to stop her mind from going back to those days. She couldn't let herself. Not now.

Alice topped up their glasses.

"Is he at least coming to the funeral?"

"I hope so." Alice shook her head but remained silent.

Paul was quickly forgotten when she told Alice about the diary she'd found. While Sarah opened another bottle of wine, Alice read the first few pages. She knew better than anyone how much it had frustrated and upset Sarah that she was kept in the dark about the past.

"Why do you think they never told you? I mean, I get that your nanna didn't want to talk about that time, I do, but why did your mum not tell you about Clara and Camille? Surely she must have been proud that her mum had done something so brave?"

"That's exactly what I've been wondering. Why didn't they want me to know that she potentially saved two people's lives? There must be a reason for that. I haven't read all of it yet. I'm hoping when I finish it, I'll know more."

Before Sarah went to bed, she sent Paul a message.

"Are you okay? Haven't heard from you. Maybe talk tomorrow? Night night x"

She put her phone on her bedside table and just before she fell asleep, she whispered as she did every night: "Sleep tight, my darling Emma."

***

Paul sat on the floor in Emma's room with one hand in her cot. Many nights he'd spent sitting in that exact same spot trying to get her off to sleep. For hours he would stroke her little hand. The lullabies he sung over and over again always calmed her down, but rarely made her fall asleep. She'd lay there and look at him with those big brown eyes that were Sarah's. If he stopped singing, she'd cry. Often it took hours before she'd finally give in and shut her eyes. He'd stay for another 15 minutes to make sure she was properly asleep. If he left too early, she'd wake up and he would have to start all over again. Praying the door wouldn't creak, he'd sneak out of her room relieved to be able to escape. He thought he'd never miss those times.

He'd been wrong. No matter how exhausting those nights had been, now he'd give anything to be able to spend night after sleepless night with her. He should have cherished every second.

"I don't know what to do, Em," he said to the empty room. "Your mum and I aren't doing too well and I don't know how to fix things between us." Paul's voice broke and he bit his lip. "She deserves better, so much better, but I just can't do it, sweetheart. When I look into her eyes, all I see is you. It hurts too much to love her. Loving her is like losing you again and again."

Chapter Nine

Amsterdam, February 1945

"Is it still snowing outside?" Clara asked.

Louise felt awful for Clara not even being able to look out the window to check on the weather.

"It stopped this morning. It must feel so strange not knowing what is going on in the outside world," Louise said looking at the shut curtains. "Do you want me to open them for a bit?"

"No, it would let the cold in. I don't mind not seeing it, it's only temporary. Soon I'll be able to take Camille outside and show her everything she's missed. Thanks to you."

Louise had just finished her warm water when both Anna and Camille started crying for food at exactly the same time. She winced and got up to get Anna but Clara stopped her with a touch on her arm.

"You sit down, I'll feed them both."

"Are you sure?" Clara nodded.

"They love feeding together and it will warm me up having them both close."

Louise helped settle the girls on Clara's lap. She didn't want to show how relieved she was. Feeding was getting more and more difficult, Anna never seemed to be getting enough milk. She was less fussy with Clara but the strain on her feeding Camille, and sometimes Anna as well, was starting to show. Louise always gave Clara a bigger portion of food than she would have herself but there was so little to go around that it hardly made a difference. Clara's cheekbones were sharply sticking out of her face and put shadows over the hollows where her cheeks once were. After feeding she often had no strength to get up. All she'd do was drink glass after glass of water until she was able to walk again. Louise had started giving Anna some broth in the morning and little bits of soaked bread when she had any but she was constantly worried not only about whether Anna was getting enough but also what she'd do if her milk dried up completely.

Why was she unable to do something as basic as feeding her own baby? Was she a bad mother? If Peter had been there he'd have told her not to be silly and that she was doing a fine job. But he wasn't and most of the time she was alone with her worries.

Louise looked at Anna and Camille all snuggled up and greedily feeding. The two girls looked so happy. Every now and then one of them would open their eyes as if to make sure the other was still there.

"I don't know how you do it, Clara. I struggle to feed just Anna and look at you feeding both of them at the same time." The feelings of failure were slowly seeping back into her heart.

"Don't be so tough on yourself, it's a lot harder than people think. It took me over two months to get the hang of it."

"But you stuck with it."

"I didn't have a choice," Clara looked down at Camille and smiled. "I was lucky that the family where I was hiding let me stay after she was born. But their children were a lot older so I had no back up and had to keep feeding her or she would have starved."

Louise wished she hadn't said anything. How could she be so ignorant? She started saying sorry but Clara wouldn't let her.

"Please, don't apologise. I like it that sometimes, even if it's just for a few minutes, we can talk about normal things and forget why we're sitting here like this. It's the one thing that keeps me going."

Before Louise could answer that she liked those moments too, there was a loud banging on the front door. The two women looked at each other, blood draining from their faces. Louise felt like she was being strangled by two ice cold hands, making it impossible to breathe.

"Give me Anna!" she hissed. Clara passed her over and dashed across the room with Camille, knocking her empty teacup off the table as she charged past it. She ran up the stairs as quickly and quietly as she could whilst shushing Camille to please not cry. Louise cursed herself under her breath for being so reckless. Would Clara get upstairs before she'd have to open the door?

Banging again. It was so loud Louise worried they'd break down her door. She rushed into the hallway and opened the front door to three German soldiers. She tried her hardest to appear calm, holding Anna tight in an attempt to steady her shaking hands. But she couldn't stop her heart from beating as loud as the bomber planes in the night. The soldiers were oblivious to the fear that was raging through her body and pushed past her nearly knocking her over.

Louise hurried after them into the dark living room where the one who was clearly in charge, had sat himself down in Peter's chair.

"Open those curtains!" He shouted at her. Louise opened them for the first time in months and noticed the muddy footprints he had left on her best rug. The other two soldiers stood near the door that led to the hallway as if they were worried she might escape from her own house. The one nearest the door looked into the hallway and up the stairs, tilting his head as if listening for a distant noise. Was that Camille crying upstairs? Did she just hear Clara shut the hatch? Anna was wailing, not happy about being taken off Clara's breast. Louise made no attempt to comfort her, happy for the extra noise, and put her in her little basket in the back room leaving the sliding doors between the two rooms open. It would be a challenge to warm the room back up afterwards as the cold that had been trapped in the closed off front room was quickly spreading through the house, but she didn't want Anna anywhere near those soldiers.

"We have news of your husband," the one in charge said. He was a scrawny little man with the angriest face Louise had ever seen. His nose was pointy and red, his face blotchy and his eyes sat so deep in their sockets she could barely see them.

"He has escaped and you need to tell us where he is."

A lightness came over Louise but she made sure she didn't show her relief. Peter had escaped? He was alive?

"I'm sorry," she said, trying to look like she meant it. "But I did not know he had escaped and I do not know where he is."

"This is a letter from our Commandant," without looking at her, he handed her an envelope with her name on it in big swirly writing.

"He wants to find him. Now. You have a week to give us his location. If you do not, there will be severe consequences for you and your family."

Louise gathered all the strength she didn't even know she had and replied with a calm steady voice. "Please tell your Commandant the moment I hear from my husband I will come and tell him personally. Now if you gentlemen will please excuse me, I need to feed my daughter."

Immediately Louise regretted mentioning her as the scrawny soldier got up and walked over to Anna's basket. He stroked her little cheek with the back of his hand. "You pretty little thing. We're going to find your father and when we do..." Louise followed close behind. She had to hold on to the back of a chair to stop herself from snatching Anna away from this evil man who came into their house threatening her family. She couldn't bear to look at him standing so close to Anna so she stared at the floor instead. And there, poking out from underneath the table, she saw the teacup that Clara had knocked over onto the floor in her rush to get upstairs, and her own cup still on the table. Two teacups. Would they notice the extra cup? When she thought the soldiers weren't looking, she gently kicked it out of sight. Then she noticed the teaspoon, the one Clara liked with the little windmill. She could only just reach it and she gave it a nudge to move it further under the table. Anxiously she looked up. The soldiers did not appear to have seen what she did and slowly she let out some of the breath she was holding. The scrawny soldier was still standing over Anna's basket and for a moment she feared he'd pick her up. She shivered at the thought and hugged her thin cardigan tight. It didn't help, this man gave her a chill that went right through her. Just as she thought she couldn't stand it any longer, he straightened up and moved away from the basket. Louise quickly snatched Anna up.

"Seven days!" he barked at her. And without another word he turned around and marched into the hallway, out of the front door, the other two not far behind.

Chapter Ten

Sarah woke early. It was still dark outside and it would take a few seconds before she'd be fully awake. Magical seconds in which the world is a happy place. Moments when your brain is still trying to figure out what is going on and, for the time being, assumes everything is fine and you're blissfully happy, just waking up to a normal day. That is until reality comes rushing towards you like a fighter jet and blasts you into the here and now.

After Emma died, Sarah suffered through this for weeks. Every morning she'd feel reality hitting her at full force. Reliving the same heart-breaking realisation every day was something she didn't think she'd ever get through. It hurt so much it felt impossible to survive for even a few seconds, let alone another whole day. Then, one morning, it was gone. She woke up immediately and fully aware of the devastating situation she and Paul were in. She no longer had that sliver of time in which everything seemed perfect. She knew this was a good thing. It was part of the grieving process and it meant that she was starting to move on. But how she missed those few seconds of happiness and wished they would come back.

She picked up her phone to check the time and saw that Paul had replied to her message an hour or so before.

"I'm okay. Busy. Talk tomorrow?"

Sarah shook her head and sighed. She knew he had a busy job but surely a 5-minute phone call wasn't too much to ask? She managed to refrain from responding with a sarcastic comment and, instead, let him know that the funeral was planned for Wednesday morning and asked if he could please come. Keeping the peace had become second nature to Sarah, but even though she was able to avoid conflict very successfully, she was unable to escape the pain that her failing marriage caused her. Did Paul really care so little about her that he'd let her deal with all this on her own? Sarah put her phone down and got up to have a shower. No point sitting here stewing over Paul, she had an outfit to buy.

It was about two miles to the city centre and there was a tram every 10 minutes ready to take her there, but after the day she'd had yesterday she needed a walk. It was a bright and crisp morning and it felt good to be outside. She took the long way so she could walk through the park. She'd always had a soft spot for parks in big cities and Het Vondelpark was by far her favourite. Walking along the path that snaked around the oval shaped park, Sarah felt truly at home. The duck ponds, the massive old trees that, in summer, protected the park's visitors from the burning sun, the open-air theatre and the parrots in their high-top homes. You could hear the city buzzing in the distance but its sounds were drowned by birdsong and the breeze softly caressing the trees. The memories of all the times she'd spent here jumped out at her from behind the trees.

The park was involved in most occasions celebrated by the people of Amsterdam. Queen's Day on the 30th April when she, and hundreds of other children, sold her old toys from a picnic blanket. And when she was a teenager, Liberation Day on the 5th of May. Sarah and her friends would spend all day and most of the night in the park celebrating their freedom and watching the bands play on the many stages set up for the event. It was also where Paul had proposed to her all those years ago, when life had been carefree and happy. They'd been over for a long weekend to visit her mum and were on their way to have a meal in the city. It was a summer's evening and there was a welcoming coolness to the air as the day had been very hot. The park was full of people relaxing on the grass, playing football or just wandering about. All of a sudden Paul had stopped, dropped down on one knee and asked Sarah the question. It was the spontaneity of the proposal that had really charmed her. Paul had been almost as surprised as she was. He didn't even have a ring. Later he'd told her that even though he'd thought about proposing a few times, he hadn't planned to do it yet. But in that moment, walking through the park he'd felt so happy that he wanted to make sure it lasted forever. It was a wonderful memory, but Sarah knew they'd never again be as happy as they were in that moment.

Coming out of the park, she resisted the temptation of the incredible Rijksmuseum because she knew, once she was inside, she'd be there all day. Wandering through the rooms full of paintings by The Masters until she would stop to stare at Rembrandt's Night Watch. She'd loved that painting ever since she'd first seen it as a little girl, looking at it for what felt like hours, taking in every little detail. The elaborate clothes of the main characters, the figure in the left-hand corner scurrying off or the lit-up face of the girl who looks so out of place. Every school holiday after that first visit, she'd beg her mum to go back to see it again. They often did and every time she discovered something on the painting that she hadn't noticed before. After Sarah moved to England it turned into their little family tradition to go to the museum during Sarah's summer visit. Now she wondered if she'd ever go to see it again.

The walk that should have only have taken her 45 minutes took over an hour. The sights and smells that used to just be part of the city now all brought back memories of her mum and the past. It made her feel sad but at the same time gave her a sense of belonging. As if she was meant to be there. At home in her own city.

The Kalverstraat, the main shopping street in the city centre, was busy even for a Friday. Sarah enjoyed the hum of conversation in so many different languages and the music of the street performers who weren't in any way put off by the cold weather. She wandered in and out of several clothes shops that all seemed to be competing to play the loudest music, but nothing caught her eye. She wanted something that reflected both her mum's and her own style. But what that something was, she had no idea.

And then suddenly she saw it. In a window of a shop she'd never even heard of, a slightly sombre looking mannequin was wearing a pair of black bootcut jeans combined with a pale blue fitted jumper. It was the perfect cross between their fashion styles.

***

Paul hadn't bothered with dinner when he came home from work. A beer was what he needed. He'd had a rough day and had left the office before 5pm for the first time ever. But his meetings were done for the day and there wasn't anything that couldn't wait until Monday.

All day long people had asked him how Sarah was coping. How she was dealing with her mum's death after all she'd been through. How it must bring back all those awful memories. Paul knew it was devastating for Sarah to lose her mum when it had only been two years since they'd said goodbye to their darling Emma. And he knew they meant well, but all he'd wanted to do was shout: What about me? I've been through it too! I lost Emma too. I was her daddy and now I am nothing! But he'd kept quiet and let the pain and anger build up inside until he was sure he couldn't keep it in any longer. So he went home.

When the second beer started to take the edge off the raw feeling in his chest, Paul went to the bedroom and opened Sarah's side of the wardrobe. He moved a pile of jumpers out of the way and stared at the box. A big, pink, plastic box with a clip-top lid. Would he, finally, be able to open it and look at the photos? All of them? Even the ones he pretended didn't exist? With slow movements, almost as if his body was resisting what he was trying to do, he took the box out of the wardrobe and carried it down to the living room. He knew that opening it meant letting in the pain. He'd start the unbearable, heart-breaking process of grieving for his little girl. Once he'd opened it there'd be no turning back. He knew he'd been ignoring it for far too long. He had to do it. And he had to do it then.

Sitting on the floor in the middle of the living room, he took off the lid and looked straight at his beautiful girl smiling her very first proper smile. He remembered taking the picture and sending it off to be printed on canvas that same evening. As soon as it arrived, a few days later, he'd put it up next to the framed picture of Sarah and himself on their wedding day. Looking at it now he experienced the same feeling of intense love he did then. It felt as if his whole body was filling up with the most comforting and satisfying substance. It was the same feeling he used to get when he cuddled Emma. But now it was mixed up with so much pain, he no longer wanted to feel it.

The picture had only been up for a few months when, on the night they came home from hospital without her, he ripped it off the wall. Sarah had been angry with him for taking it down. She didn't understand, or perhaps he didn't explain that if he had any chance of surviving this, it wouldn't happen with his heart shattering to pieces every time he saw that smile. He looked at the wall, the hook was still there. Now, after all this time, he was ready to let the pain in. He kissed Emma's beautiful smile and put her back on the wall where she belonged and where she should have been all along. Next in the box were some framed photos which had also been only so briefly allowed to brighten up their house. Paul took them all out of the box and put them to one side. He would find a space for every single one of them later.

But first he had to look at the laptop. It was at the bottom of the box, covered by prints that Sarah must have ordered after Emma died as he'd never seen them before. He looked at the laptop as if he was eyeing up an opponent in a fight. It was his old laptop and it held all the photos they took in the four blissfully happy months they had with Emma. The day after the funeral he'd put it in the box and bought a new laptop to avoid looking at the photos. The happy ones and those others. He took it out of the box and plugged in the charger. His finger hovered over the power button for a few seconds, as if waiting for a countdown. Then he pressed it. While the laptop whirred to life, Paul went to the kitchen for another beer. He drank one with the fridge door still open and brought another one into the living room with him. When he sat back down the laptop was on. It was time. The number of photos was overwhelming. There must have been over a hundred just of Emma's first moments. Paul stopped at one of Sarah looking straight at him with Emma in her arms. She looked exhausted but happier than ever. Labour had lasted 26 long hours and she'd refused any pain relief as she was worried about the effects it could have on the baby. When Emma was finally born, Paul couldn't stop taking photos. The way Sarah looked at their little girl was one of the most beautiful things he had ever seen.

Paul spent hours looking at the photos, scrolling from one image to the next. Often going back to look at some of them again. It was like seeing her grow in fast forward. But the further on through the photos he got, the slower he went. He was scared of what he would see and of what would happen after that. The next photo was one of his favourites. It was a close-up of him holding Emma. She was looking him straight in the eye and was smiling. They both were. Sarah had taken it on their first and only holiday with the three of them. They went to The Peak District and spent a week strolling through the stunning countryside and having endless picnics. It was the happiest week of his life. He stared at the photo a long time before he clicked on the next button. And then there they were.

***

The last time Paul had rushed home from hospital to quickly get some things for Emma and Sarah, one of the nurses had stopped him on his way out. It was the nice one with the kind eyes who was always so gentle with Emma. The one who made cups of tea for them in the middle of the night and who would sit with them patiently answering all their questions.

"Bring your camera, Mr Fisher," she said, touching his arm as if to mark the importance of her words. Paul had been in such a daze from exhaustion that he didn't even think to wonder why she'd said it. He had gone home, found the stuff his girls needed and packed the camera and charger.

Back in hospital it had only been on charge for a little while when a nurse came in and, without disturbing the scene, took photos of Emma's final moments.

Paul looked at them through squinted eyes. He made himself see every single one of them, his heart silently screaming the whole time. The last few pictures were taken after Emma had stopped breathing. They had changed her nappy for the last time and dressed her in her little purple leggings and spotted dress and then held her until it was time to say goodbye. The nurse who came to take her away from them wrapped her gently in a soft blanket before picking her up and leaving the room. The last photo was of him and Sarah together, after they'd taken Emma away. They stood opposite each other with their foreheads touching. Tears flowing uninterrupted.

Chapter Eleven

Amsterdam, February 1945

"Are you sure this is a good idea?" Clara asked as she tied the little strings of Anna's hat under Camille's chin and made sure her cardigan was done up. She stroked her little girl's cheek and tucked the blanket in the sides of the pram.

"Yes, it will do her good to be outside. I'd take you as well if I could." Louise said.

"But what if someone notices?"

"They won't," Louise said. "Nobody really talks to each other anymore. It's like everyone's world has shrunk to only their families and most trusted friends. People who used to say hello in passing, now walk past each other as if they've never met before."

"But her eyes, she's got my brown eyes whilst Anna's couldn't be bluer if they tried."

"Don't worry. She'll probably fall asleep as soon as we start moving anyway." Clara still didn't look convinced.

"Trust me," Louise said and stroked Anna's chin who was happy enough in Clara's arms. "See you later, poppet. Be good."

With Camille so wrapped up, it was tricky to tell the difference, but still, eyes and ears waiting to betray seemed to be everywhere these days. She put Anna's bunny closer to Camille's cheek and started humming the lullaby that always sent Anna off to sleep in the pram hoping it would work with Camille as well. Louise ignored the urge to constantly look around for people she knew and kept her head down. Better to be seen as rude than risk being found out, she thought.

Even though it was cold, there was no wind and if you ignored the snow, you could almost be fooled to think spring was on its way. The queue for food was long today. You knew you'd be waiting a long time when the queue snaked around the corner like it did now. She was relieved to see Mrs van Dijk was already further towards the front of the queue. Soon she'd turn the corner and be out of sight. If anyone was going to notice it would be Mrs van Dijk, who sometimes looked after Anna for her, Louise just hoped she wouldn't stop to chat on the way back. Camille's big brown eyes, such a contrast with the blue of Peter's and her own, were wide open taking in all the unknown sights. All she could do was pray that nobody noticed.

Apart from Mrs van Dijk, who, to Louise's relief, waved apologetically for not stopping, she didn't see many familiar faces, and none that she knew well enough for them to approach and chat. She felt drained of energy and was happy to be back home. But when she handed Camille back to Clara, she was sure she could see a little colour had returned to Camille's pale little face.

Chapter Twelve

"It was a beautiful service, Sarah," Alice said as they were waiting outside for Paul to get the car.

"Do you think she'd have been happy with it?"

"More than happy. You really did her proud. It was all in her style and she would have loved that you led the service and not some funeral director she'd never met. It was perfect."

"I'll miss you," Sarah said trying hard not to let any more tears escape.

"Me too, it's been nice having you back for a while. It felt like good old times. Are you coming back soon to sort out the house?"

"Yes, hopefully in a few weeks' time depending on work and Paul." The mention of Paul lacked commitment but Alice didn't comment. Sarah gave her a hug.

"Well, let me know, I'll have wine ready." Alice wasn't one for soppy goodbyes, she was always the one joking while Sarah tried not to cry but today her cheerful tone sounded fake. "Look your ride's here," she said as she peeled Sarah's arms from around her neck.

"See you soon, Alice," Sarah said as she got into car.

"Sure thing. I'll be here."

On the way to the airport it was Paul who, so unlike him, made conversation to try and break the deadly silence that shrouded them. Sarah's one-word answers didn't add much to his efforts and he gave up long before they'd returned the hire car and queued up to check in. For once Sarah, who had never liked travelling by plane, was pleased he'd insisted on flying instead of the long ferry journey that took over 7 hours. Soon they'd be in the air and on their way home but Sarah couldn't shake the feeling that she was walking away from the place where she was meant to be.

***

As soon as she walked through the front door of the house that once felt like home, Sarah noticed something was different. As if the energy had changed. When she left for Amsterdam the atmosphere had been oppressive and dark. Now, despite the awkward silence that they couldn't seem to shake, she sensed a more open, almost peaceful, vibe. It surprised her and even though it felt good, she was not comforted by it.

"I've got to show you something," Paul said in a caring tone that she was no longer used to. She followed him into the living room and immediately her eyes were drawn to the photo. Her beautiful girl, smiling at them both.

"You put her back up," Sarah said without taking her eyes of Emma's smile.

"I did. I thought it was time."

Sarah turned towards Paul but failed to catch his eye. A knot was slowly forming in her stomach.

"So does that mean you…?" for a long time she'd been desperate to hear the answer to the question she now didn't dare ask.

"I did. I looked at them. All of them."

Ever since Emma died, Sarah had encouraged Paul to look at the photos. They had helped her learn acknowledge the pain and deal with it and she was convinced it would help him as well. She'd learned to expect the range of emotions when she broached the subject. Mostly he'd decline politely or sigh and ignore her all together but every now and then he would shout at her to leave him alone. Whatever his reaction, never did she think he was going to look at them. He just seemed to pretend they didn't exist.

"They're beautiful and I'm so glad I've seen them. I'm sorry, Sarah, you were right all along. I should have looked at them ages ago." Sarah felt a but coming.

"I should have dealt with this way earlier but now I've seen the photos I have no choice, I have to come to terms with it."

"I know. And I'm here for you, just as you were for me. Whatever you need."

"Space," he said so quietly Sarah barely noticed he'd said anything at all. "I need space." Sarah wobbled on her feet. She tried to grab Paul's hand but he pulled it out of her reach.

"What do you mean you need space?"

"I need to do this on my own. I need space to do this my way, with nobody around. Not even you."

Sarah felt a rush of dizziness go to her head. She stumbled to the sofa and sat down. Paul still stood staring at Emma's picture.

"You won't let me help you?"

"I'm sorry, Sarah, I know you're going through a hard time and I wish I'd listened to you sooner. But I have to do this now and I can't do it when I'm around you. When you're here, all I see is her. It suffocates me, the pain, the love, the loss. I push it away because it would kill me if I didn't. I need to do this slowly. Without you being a constant reminder of what we've lost."

Sarah tried to slow down her breathing. Her heart was ready to explode into a thousand razor-sharp shards of anger and pain. Finally, he was ready to do what she'd wanted him to for so long. The thing she'd always thought would save their marriage. And now he wanted to do it without her. Sarah got up and walked out of the room.

"Where are you going?"

She stopped in the doorway and looked him in the eye. She couldn't sleep next to him knowing he didn't want her there. Knowing he wanted to do this without her when he had done so much to help her.

"I'm sleeping in Emma's room tonight."

Chapter Thirteen

Amsterdam, February 1945

Every few seconds Louise checked the big clock on the church tower. It had only been 10 minutes since she'd left without Anna but it felt more like an hour. She had this uncomfortable feeling in her stomach as if she was forgetting something important. She knew it was because she'd not been out of the house on her own since Anna was born, but still she couldn't shake it. Apart from the time she'd taken Camille, Anna always came with her to get rations. But today it was so cold that she worried about taking her outside. Sometimes the queues were endless and you could be waiting for hours. She was grateful when Clara had offered to look after her. Even though it hadn't been easy leaving the house without her, she knew it was the right thing to do. Every time Louise took a breath, the icy air hurt her lungs. The canal she walked past to get to the shops was frozen solid and, were this a happier time, the scene would have been that of children learning to ice-skate, pushing wooden chairs out in front of them to help them balance. Louise remembered when her father first took her ice-skating, not far from there. He'd bought her a pair of second-hand wooden skates which he'd tied under her shoes with leather straps. They'd brought the little chair from her bedroom to help her balance and after a wobbly start, she shuffled forwards pushing the chair ahead of her whilst her father skated to the bridge, about 100 yards away, and back again. When she finally got close to the bridge herself, her father helped her turn around.

"You don't want to skate under the bridge, Lou," he said cupping his hands around his mouth and blowing warm air into them. "The ice is not strong enough yet."

How he'd known that she had no idea, but she didn't doubt it for a second. Her father always knew everything that was worth knowing. When her hands were stiff from the cold, they went back home where her mother was waiting with a cup of hot milk and honey, two teaspoons to make it extra sweet.

If only life could be so simple now. She looked up at the clock again. Only a minute had passed. Louise shivered and took a step forward as the long line of people moved almost unnoticeably.

She knew that Clara would be pleased to finally be able to help by looking after Anna. They talked yesterday about how she felt so useless sitting in that freezing attic all day long. Clara tried to do whatever she could to help, but she said nothing could ever come close enough to repaying her for what she had done for them. Louise told her all she wanted in return was for them to live, but she did understand how Clara felt. She'd feel the same.

She pulled up her collar to try and keep warm but it was no use. Her coat had seen better days and wasn't anywhere near warm enough for that kind of weather. Her scarf, a Christmas present from Peter, was far less cosy and warm than when she'd unwrapped it over six years ago. She had such fond memories of that day. They'd gotten married a few weeks before and it was their first Christmas in their own house. They'd gotten up early so they had time to open each other's gifts before both their parents were due to arrive. The beautifully soft and thick scarf had been such a thoughtful gift to Louise who was always cold. She loved how it used to tickle her cheek before it had worn thin. When she'd read the accompanying note, she had tears in her eyes.

To keep you warm, even when I'm not around.
All my love,
Peter.

Back then, they'd had no idea how appropriate that message would become.

"Morning, Louise. Have you heard from Peter yet?"

Louise had been so distracted by the happy memory that she hadn't noticed Frank walking up to her. She looked at him and squinted her eyes slightly. Why was he asking after Peter? What did he know?

"Morning, Frank," she said trying to keep her tone light. "No, not yet but hopefully he will be home soon."

"I hope so too, Louise. It can't be easy for you on your own." Frank pulled his cap down so low, she could barely see his bright blue eyes. Piercing eyes that always seemed to be scanning for, Louise didn't know what.

"I cope, Frank, we all do."

"We sure do. If you need any jobs doing around the house make sure you let me know. I'm always happy to help. You know that, don't you?"

"I know, but I'm alright really. Thank you though." Louise wished he would just get on with his business and leave her to hers. He was a nice enough man but far too nosy for her liking. It always seemed like he was prying for information. There was a rumour going around that Frank had betrayed several Jewish families hiding in the neighbourhood. Louise wasn't normally one to pay attention to gossip, but with Clara and Camille at home she couldn't be too careful. She hated how mistrusting this war had made her and could imagine Peter telling her not to listen to the women's chatter but she had no choice. She had to keep Anna safe. Finally, it looked like Frank was going to leave.

"You have a nice day, Louise. Please let me know if I can help in any way. And don't you worry about Peter."

Louise didn't like the way he was looking at her, as if he was trying to read her mind.

"Thank you, Frank, you have a good day too," she said with a nod, relieved that the conversation was over and he was walking away from her. But then, just as she started to relax a little, he turned back to face her.

"Where is Anna this morning?"

For a moment Louise was unable to speak. Her throat tightened and her mouth became so dry it was difficult to swallow. She should have been prepared for this. She should have had an excuse ready. She pulled at her scarf to loosen it. She needed to breathe. Breathe and talk. Say something, anything. After a silence that lasted so long it surely must have raised his suspicion, she finally spoke.

"Mrs van Dijk from next door is looking after her. Anna has been a little poorly and I didn't want to bring her out in the cold today. It's only for a little while so I can get our rations." Louise had to make a conscious effort to stop talking.

"Sorry to hear little Anna is under the weather. Get the doctor to have a look at her, make sure it's nothing serious."

"I will do," she said willing him to turn around.

When he finally walked off, Mrs van Dijk opened her front door and stepped outside. She waved at Louise who started shaking. She didn't dare wave back and just nodded and tried to smile. She couldn't move. From the corner of her eye she saw Frank turn around and look at Mrs van Dijk with no poorly Anna in her arms. Louise turned her back to both of them and held on to a lamp post.

Chapter Fourteen

On the ferry, the queue for the lift was far too long for Sarah's already dwindled patience. Seven floors she had to go up. She looked at her suitcases, winced, took a deep breath and started dragging them up the first flight. The violin case she carried over her shoulder slipped off a little more with each step.

"Just six more floors," she said to herself after climbing up just one.

When she had made it to the 4th floor she stopped for a minute to catch her breath. "Make mental note: Go running more often. You are seriously unfit, Mrs Fisher." The days that Sarah and Paul would go running together every Sunday morning were long gone. With little enthusiasm, Sarah picked up her cases again. She couldn't wait to sit down with a cup of coffee. Looking up at the next flight of stairs she saw a man leaning on the balustrade. When he saw Sarah, he smiled and for a moment she didn't feel the weight of her luggage.

"Oh, hello," she said, her cheeks heating up. "Sorry, I was just talking to myself."

"Yeah, I got that." He had one of those wonky smiles. The slightest imperfection in an otherwise perfectly handsome face. Sarah felt the start of a sheepish grin which would soon spread all over her face. She tried to stop it but it wouldn't be held back. Once again she felt like the awkward teenager she used to be. All blushing cheeks, weird smile and no idea what to say.

"You want help with those suitcases? They look heavy."

"They are but I can manage," Sarah said with a sharpness she didn't mean. The effect this stranger had on her made her undecided between wanting to run away as fast as she could and being as close to him as possible.

"I'm sure you can," a twinkle in his eye. "You're a strong independent woman, right?" She liked his forwardness. And his pale blue eyes. They were hypnotising and hard to look away from. Looking up at him she felt something in the gut of her stomach. Butterflies? Surely not.

"Fine, mock me if it makes you feel more manly." She softened the remark with a smile. She expected a cheeky response but he just stood there without saying a word. After a few seconds of looking at each other, which Sarah surprisingly noticed weren't awkward, he picked up his backpack.

"Well then, you have a nice day." He turned around and started up the stairs.

Sarah's arms ached. She didn't want him to go, she wanted his help.

"Okay, okay!" Sarah shouted up at him laughing. "If you insist, you can carry my suitcases!" She was relieved to see him walking back down towards her, cheeky grin and all. He bent down to pick up her suitcases and winked at her on his way back up. He came so close, she could smell his aftershave. It smelled fresh, as if he'd just had a shower. She inhaled the scent as you would a freshly brewed cup of coffee. As he turned his back to her she noticed his broad shoulders and his tall frame.

"I'm Jack by the way. It's nice to meet you seriously unfit, Mrs Fisher."

Sarah racked her brain for something witty to say but Jack was already halfway up the stairs, taking two steps at a time.

***

A couple of weeks after Paul had told her he needed space, Sarah got fed up with doing 'the awkward dance of avoidance' and decided to go back to Holland for a while. Paul clearly didn't want her there and no matter how much it had hurt her when he told her he couldn't move on with her around, she did understand. And after the way he'd helped her get back on her feet, she felt she owed it to him to return the favour, even if that meant taking a break from each other. So, she packed two big suitcases and booked a ferry ticket. She contacted her students to tell them that she wouldn't be around for some time. For the first time, she felt relieved she wasn't performing anymore. It was unlikely the orchestra would have let her go without any notice. Since she'd quit, shortly after Emma died, she'd been trying to make herself believe that teaching was the best thing for her.

Her head knew she'd made the right decision but she hadn't yet been able to convince her heart that still yearned for the buzz of performing and the satisfying sound of the applause.

She was heartbroken and had never felt more alone. But there was also another feeling trying to slither its way to the surface. It was faint but clearly present. It whispered that this was the right thing to do. She had no real plan other than to start sorting through her mum's things and probably, at some point, put the house up for sale. Although she was upset, she was also looking forward to being on her own for a while. Not having to worry about what Paul's mood would be like when he came home from work and not having to bite her tongue to avoid an argument.

And there was another reason she was keen to get back to her mum's house. After the funeral they'd gone back to England straight away so Paul wouldn't miss another day at work and in her rush to pack she'd forgotten to bring her nanna's diary. She couldn't wait to read the rest of it.

***

"Thank you," Sarah said as Jack held the door to her cabin open for her. She fully intended to shut it on him and keep it closed until she could see the beach of Hoek van Holland but something stopped her, made her linger in the doorway.

"Would you like to join me for an ice cream?" Jack asked.

"An ice cream?"

"Yes. You know those cold creamy things that people eat in summer."

"But it's February…"

"True. And if I thought it would've worked, I'd have asked you for a coffee. But that would have been boring and far too easy to decline." Jack held his hand out to Sarah. "Ice cream on the other hand got your attention and I'm hoping you're so baffled by the ridiculous suggestion that you will say yes. Even if it is out of pure confusion."

Sarah smiled and, ignoring all her instincts and feelings of loyalty towards Paul, she took his hand.

"Okay then. Ice cream it is."

"So, Mrs Fisher," Jack said in between bites of his ice cream sandwich.

"Please, call me Sarah."

"Okay, Sarah, I have two questions for you."

They were leaning against the railing at the back of the ship watching England disappear in the distance. It was cold, far too cold for ice cream, but Sarah welcomed the fresh air and the company. There weren't many people on the outside deck. Only a few smokers huddled together at the little tables near the doors, desperately sucking in the nicotine before running back inside.

"Ask away."

"What is a beautiful woman like you, with enough luggage to last a good few weeks, doing on a ferry on her own?" From the corner of her eye Sarah noticed that Jack briefly looked at her wedding ring.

"And why did you choose a rocket lolly?" Sarah laughed out loud for what felt like the first time in years.

"I like rocket lollies," she said, gently bumping his arm with her shoulder.

"Kids like rocket lollies," Jack said and Sarah laughed again.

"Yes, they do and maybe that is why I like them." Jack looked at her as if she was a book he was desperate to read. He waited for her to explain.

"My mum used to buy me a rocket lolly every Friday after school, even in the middle of winter, and she would have one as well. If it was warm enough, we would sit down on a bench overlooking a playground near our house and when we finished our lollies, I would play until it was time to go in for dinner. If it rained, we would run home with our lollies and eat them in front of the tv." It felt good to talk about her mum with a stranger and the happy memory made her smile.

"One Friday I asked her whether she wouldn't rather have a different ice cream like a Cornetto or a Magnum or something else a bit more grown-up." Sarah's voice trembled a little. "But she told me she wanted just this, nothing else, it was perfect."

"She sounds great."

"She is. She was. She passed away a few weeks ago, which I guess answers your other question. I'm going home to Amsterdam to sort out her house."

"I'm sorry, Sarah." Jack took her hand and squeezed it gently. Sarah stared out to sea blinking hard to clear her blurry vision.

"That doesn't answer all of it though." Sarah looked at him wondering what he was getting at. "It explains why you're here but not why you're alone." That last word felt like a punch in Sarah's stomach.

"I would have thought that, given the circumstances, you would perhaps have your husband with you to, at least, carry your ridiculously heavy suitcases." Sarah smiled but the joy Jack had seen in her eyes earlier was gone.

"He needed some space."

Jack didn't say anything but moved a bit closer and let Sarah lean into him as he ate his ice cream.

Later that day Sarah sat in her cabin watching the sunlight reflect on the waves. She was mesmerised by the little sparkles of light bouncing from one wave to the next. The light was so bright it hurt her eyes but she couldn't look away. It had been an unexpectedly good day. She'd spent most of it with Jack and was surprised at how relaxed she felt in his company. He made her laugh and when he came close she felt something that had been dormant for years. Should she have asked for his phone number? She almost had but a glimpse of the ring on her left hand had stopped her. She knew it had been the right decision but that didn't stop her regretting it.

Her thoughts were interrupted by the sound of several text messages arriving on her phone.

"I guess we're nearly there then." When she got her phone out of her coat pocket something fell out. She picked it up. It was a business card she'd never seen before.

Jack Rogers
Carpentry and Decorating

Sarah turned the card over and smiled at the message scribbled on the back.

Call me. If you want. Jack x

Chapter Fifteen

Amsterdam, February 1945

It was the cold that had woken Louise up early. She'd gone to bed in all of her clothes but that still hadn't been enough to keep her warm. Her legs ached with stiffness when she shuffled around for her slippers. She picked Anna up from her cot and held her close. She slept on despite the cold. Knowing that the only chance she had to warm up a little was to move, she went downstairs. In the back room it was a touch warmer but she could still see her breath. Hopefully the weather would improve soon, it felt like winter had been going on forever.

Louise put Anna in her basket and bent down to touch the leaves and sticks she'd found the day before and put in front of the stove. They weren't completely dry, but if she rolled them into a few pages of a book, she might be able to light them. It wouldn't be enough to boil water, but maybe it could at least warm up the little bit of soup she'd saved from last night's dinner. Clara would need something to warm her up that morning. If she was this cold after sleeping in a bed, she could only imagine what it was like on the attic floor.

Louise and Clara hadn't had their afternoon cup of tea in the back room for a few days now. They were scared, it had been too close an escape. Clara and Camille had stayed in the attic leaving Louise lonely and worried for their wellbeing. She'd make sure to get them to come down later today for a warm drink and a chat. Louise put the soup on the stove and got on with her morning chores.

The knock on the door made her yelp. Every little sound made her jump since those awful soldiers had knocked on her door. Even when she was expecting someone and she knew Clara and Camille were safely in the attic, a knock would leave her shaking with fear.

"Please, don't let it be those soldiers again," she muttered under her breath as she wrapped Anna in a blanket, took a deep breath and went to the door. Although relieved to see there were no soldiers knocking on her door, she wasn't all that thrilled with her unexpected visitor.

"Morning, Frank, what brings you here?" Louise tried to keep the distrust out of her voice but very much doubted she managed it. She had always believed in thinking the best of people unless they proved you otherwise but it was so hard now to know who you could and, more importantly, couldn't trust. People you'd known for years suddenly turned out to be traitors. It was impossible to be sure of who your true friends were.

A couple of days before she'd met Martha, one of her school friends she'd known since she was 6, and started chatting. They used to play at each other's houses all the time and they kept in touch after they left school. Louise had always thought her a kind friend but she'd been shocked when Martha said she was happy that there wouldn't be so many Jews around anymore, stealing good people's jobs and eating their food. Louise nodded silently and cut down the conversation as soon as she could. She'd walked away without her rations and had to return later when there was hardly anything left. Friends and enemies all had the same face. There was no telling them apart. Still, traitor or not, she'd rather have Frank at her door than soldiers.

"Hello, Louise, I just wanted to check how little Anna was doing and see if you needed anything."

There was something in his eyes that made her want to tell him as little as possible.

"She's fine, Frank, it turned out to be just a cold. We worried over nothing really."

"We? Is Peter back home?" Frank tried to look around Louise into the hallway as if he expected to see him appear from the front room.

Louise couldn't believe it. Again she almost misspoke in front of Frank, but this time she was a bit quicker to answer. With a steady voice and holding Anna tight to hide her shaking hands, she replied.

"No, I wish he was, Frank, it's just me and Anna." Could she hear Clara moving around upstairs? "I'm sorry Frank but Anna didn't sleep very well last night because of her cold so please forgive me for being rude, but I would really like to go back inside for a rest."

"Of course, of course. I could come in and help you with Anna for a bit of you like? You can have a rest then. It can't be easy doing all of this on your own with only Mrs van Dijk to help out." Why did he mention Mrs van Dijk? Was it because she lied to him the other day? Was he fishing for information? Louise's legs started to wobble.

"That's very kind of you, Frank, but no, thank you. I really must go in and feed her."

"Of course, you get yourself inside Louise." Frank leaned in closer. "Do you have enough food? Or do you need anything for Anna?" he whispered. Why was he asking that? Did he suspect she was hiding someone?

"We're really fine, Frank," keeping her tone as calm as possible. "We're hungry, but who isn't? If there is anything going spare, which I doubt, I'm sure there are people who'd need it far more than we do."

"You are a good soul, Louise, Peter will be so proud of you when he comes back." If he comes back, Louise quietly added in her head.

"At least let me give you this." Frank took something out of his pocket and put it in Louise's hand. "Maybe you should get your sewing box out and make something for Anna." He looked her straight in the eye when he said this, Louise felt shivers racing up and down her spine. She had to get him out of there. When he turned around and stepped away from the door she shut it quickly and looked at what he had given her. It was a red handkerchief with white flowers in the middle and a border of leaves around the edges. The kind that farmers wore around their necks.

Chapter Sixteen

"How long are you staying?" Alice asked. Sarah had texted her on the ferry with the news that she was on her way back to Amsterdam. They'd arranged to meet for dinner that same evening. Sarah craved her friend's easy company in which she could be herself completely. Over a cool glass of wine, she'd updated Alice on the situation with Paul.

"Could be a week, a month, forever. I have no idea. We didn't really talk about the specifics. He just said he needed space."

"So, are you splitting up?"

"When I left this morning I didn't think so, but," Sarah thought about how to phrase what she wanted to say. "It's almost a relief not being around him." Alice smiled. "It's only been a day but already I feel more re-laxed, like I can breathe again. As if I have more space around me. "

"I'll drink to that," Alice said holding up her glass. "Welcome home, Sarah." Alice was right. She was home.

She had no idea what would happen with her and Paul but for now she was just happy to be home.

"Do you know what the weirdest thing is about being here?" Alice looked up from the burger and chips she'd been devouring.

"Emma's never been here. I've lived here most of my life and she never even got to visit or stay at my mum's house. It feels like she has no connection, no place here. Does that make sense?"

"It does. So why don't you make a place for her. Paint a room the same colour as her nursery or plant a tree in the garden." Alice could always be counted on for the most practical solution to an emotional problem.

"I like the idea of a tree, maybe I'll do that."

Seeing Alice had done Sarah good. Despite her over-all melancholy mood, she felt a hint of positivity. Her heart was breaking for her marriage but being there, feeling the last wisps of her mum's presence was com-forting. Even though she was tired from travelling all day, she didn't feel like going to bed yet. The box with her nanna's diary was still on the bookshelf, silently en-couraging her to find out what happened next. Sarah made herself comfortable in her mum's favourite chair and continued reading where she'd left off.

After just over an hour of deciphering the tiny handwriting Sarah shut the diary.

"What?" she said louder than she meant to. "That doesn't make any sense." When she'd passed the halfway point of the notebook the writing had suddenly stopped. Sarah flicked through the remaining pages as if to look for a secret entry she might have missed. But there wasn't another word to be found. She looked up without focusing on anything in particular, shaking her head and muttering to herself. Why would she stop writing? There were plenty of blank pages left. Why not continue? She'd religiously written something every single day. Sometimes it was only a couple of sentences and every now and then she wrote just one word. Scared, Hungry or Cold. But there was something for every day. There must have been some reason she gave up. It can't have been that there was nothing to write about, the war would go on for another couple of months at least. And she couldn't imagine that she'd have just lost interest in writing. Sarah herself had started a diary after Emma died to help her come to terms with her death and it had been a great comfort to her, it still was. She no longer wrote every day but rarely a week went by without her feeling the need to put her thoughts down on paper. Her nanna must have felt something similar. The pleasure of sharing your thoughts, even with a piece of paper, the feeling of having someone to talk to when you feel so alone must have helped her through that darkest time. But why not continue? Maybe there was something she didn't want to trust to anyone, not even her diary. Writing things down made them real, which was one of the reasons it had helped Sarah so much. Once it was on paper there was no longer a way of denying it. Maybe something happened that her nanna didn't want to be made real? Was it something that happened to Clara? Or Camille? And the only person who might be able to tell her was Camille. Was she still alive? And if she was, would Sarah be able to find her?

"Why didn't you tell me, Mum? Why leave me with all these questions?"

Determined to find some answers the following day, Sarah went to bed. She'd decided not to sleep in her teenage room again but in the quieter guest bedroom at the back of the house. The one she used when she came to visit with Paul. It was a much calmer room and it didn't feel so drenched in memories.

***

To reach the attic hatch, Sarah took the old wooden chair from her mum's bedroom. It looked about a hundred years old and wobbled as she stepped on it. A cold breeze tickled her neck as she reached up to open it. She wondered if this was the same chair her nanna had used to get up there. The hatch opened easily but with a loud creak. Sarah reached for the ladder that she knew would be near the opening. It was an old-fashioned stepladder that had definitely seen better days. She moved the chair out of the way, balanced the ladder and started the unsteady climb up.

"I wouldn't like to do this in a hurry," she said to herself as she stepped off the ladder onto the attic floor. She let her eyes adjust to the darkness. There was only one little window in the back wall to light up the whole space. The insulation that her mum had put in years ago hadn't stopped it from being cold and she couldn't begin to imagine how cold it must have been up there during the war. Sarah looked around and tried to remember whether her mum had ever used the attic for storage or anything else but she couldn't remember ever seeing anything up there. The builders, who put the insulation in, had commented on how they'd never seen such a big attic with so little stuff in it. She hadn't thought much of it at the time but now she saw the empty space, knowing what had happened up there, things slowly started making sense.

Every year, just before the end of the summer holiday, Sarah's mum made her clear out her room and bag up everything she no longer wanted and any clothes she'd grown out of. This big summer tidy up wasn't limited to her room, the whole house was subject to it. Bags of clothes that were too small, toys that had become unwanted and videos that were no longer watched were all taken to a charity shop. Nothing was kept. Nothing was stored. Sarah never understood why her mum was so obsessed with keeping only what they needed and getting rid of everything else. But now she wondered whether it perhaps had less to do with tidiness and more with not wanting to go up into the attic. She flicked through her childhood memories but couldn't remember ever seeing her mum go up that ladder so she wasn't surprised to only find one small cardboard box covered in years of dust. She moved it near the hatch ready to take down.

Sarah slowly walked around touching the low beams and imagining Clara and Camille living up there day in day out in the freezing cold. She tried to picture what the room would have looked like with the makeshift bed in the middle, the bucket Clara used as a toilet and maybe some books to keep her occupied during the day. She walked over to the window, ducking out of the way of the beams, and noticed four tiny holes in the window frame. She touched each one with her index finger as if to signify their importance. Those holes must have been from the pins that held up the piece of fabric her grandmother had put up to stop her guests from being seen. It was the only visible proof of what had happened there over 70 years ago.

Chapter Seventeen

Amsterdam, February 1945

As soon as Anna had gone down for a nap Louise sat in front of the stove and rested her eyes. She was exhausted but far too anxious to sleep. Frank's unexpected knock on her door had made her feel uneasy. Thoughts raced around in her head. What was the reason for his visit? Was he snooping around, trying to catch her out? Or was he one of the good guys who just wanted to help and who could really get her more rations? Unable to calm her worried mind, she went to get the broom out of her wardrobe upstairs and knocked on the ceiling. It didn't take long for Clara to open the hatch and let down the stepladder. She was shivering and had dark shadows under her eyes.

"Are you sure it's safe?" she whispered. In Clara's eyes, Louise could see the guilt she felt for putting her and Anna at risk. Louise wished she could make her understand that she owed her nothing. That without Clara to share her experiences with, she didn't know how she'd get through this endless winter.

"As safe as ever," Louise said with a smile.

Clara climbed down the stepladder with Camille sleeping in her arms and gave Louise a hug.

"You look exhausted, Clara, maybe you should sleep in my bed tonight," she said as they drank their cup of warm water in the back room. Louise longed for a hot cup of tea or coffee, but at least the drink was warm and she had Clara's company to enjoy.

"I can sleep in my chair and Camille can snuggle up with Anna."

"It's too risky," Clara said even though the look in her eyes betrayed her longing feeling for a soft and reasonably warm bed. "What if they come in the night and I can't get upstairs quick enough? I can't let you put yourself and Anna in even more danger. You're already risking too much for us."

"Anyone decent would have done the same." Louise said looking down at her lap.

"You know that's not true. There are plenty of people who ignore the suffering of others. Many wouldn't have even come to the door, let alone open it." Louise thought of her friend Martha and knew Clara was right.

"Maybe, but you're helping me too. I think I would have gone mad if I didn't have you to talk to and to help look after Anna. I know it sounds strange, but, especially with Peter gone, it is wonderful having you here."

Clara played with the teaspoon in her cup. They didn't have any sugar to stir but Louise still put a spoon in every hot drink.

"We owe you our lives and, one day, I will repay that enormous debt."

"There is no debt, Clara, you have nothing to repay. As long as you and Camille are safe, that's all that matters to me."

Anna stirred and Louise went to have a look. Right next to Anna's little face was the handkerchief that Frank had given her earlier. Louise picked it up and shivered, still worried about his real intentions for dropping by.

"What's that?" Clara asked when she saw Louise's reaction to it.

"I'm not sure really." She told Clara about Frank's visit. "He asked a few too many questions for my liking and then, out of the blue, he gave me this." She handed the handkerchief to Clara. "He said I should get my sewing kit out and make something for Anna."

"That's a bit strange, why would he say that?"

"I don't know. I have a bad feeling about it, Clara, I'm worried he's been far too nosy lately." Clara didn't appear to be listening, she was having a close look at the handkerchief and ran her fingers along the pattern at the edges. All of a sudden she stopped and held it up in the air.

"Look at this," she said. "The hem on this side is a right mess. It's much wider than the others and all wonky. It looks like my husband's stitched it together."

Clara laughed, but Louise jumped up as if stung by a bee and started rummaging in the sideboard for her sewing kit. She snatched the handkerchief out of Clara's hands and rushed back to her seat. With her seam ripper she started unpicking the messy hem. As soon as she got a few of the stitches out she saw what looked like a rolled-up piece of paper.

"There's something in here!" Clara leaned closer across the table and looked as Louise rushed to take out all the wonky stitches without damaging the fabric. She took out the piece of paper that had been sewn into it and unrolled it. When she read the scribbled message, she brought her hand up to her open mouth.

"What is it?"

"It's from Peter. It's a note from Peter."

"What does it say?" Louise read the short message three times before she could read it out loud to Clara.

I'm in hiding. But I am well. Be careful but trust Frank. He will help. Love to you and Anna. You are in my dreams every night.

Peter.

p.s. burn this message

"He's alive, Clara! He's alive and well." Clara and Louise hugged each other, both with tears in their eyes.

"I can't believe he managed to get a message to me." Then her face dropped.

"Oh no," she said.

"What's the matter?" Clara asked.

"Poor Frank. I've been treating him like a filthy traitor when all that time he has been trying to tell me Peter was safe. How terrible."

"I'm sure he'll understand." Clara said. "He probably knows better than anyone how hard it is to know who to trust. It's impossible. One of my best friends, whom I've known my whole life, has betrayed several Jewish families, whilst the boy who bullied me in school arranged my first hiding place for me. The world has been turned upside down." Louise still looked worried. "He'll understand, I know he will."

"I'm so glad you're here, Clara."

"So am I, Louise. So am I."

Chapter Eighteen

The content of the box was disappointing at best. Sarah knew it was silly to expect this small box to hold all the answers she was looking for but she had hoped for a little more than what she'd found. There were some of Sarah's old baby clothes, all things she guessed her nanna would have knitted. She smiled at the orange and brown dress that couldn't be more seventies if it tried. She took the rest of the baby clothes out and decided pretty quickly that there wasn't anything worth keeping. The last thing in the box was the baby blanket her nanna had knitted for her mum just after the war and was then passed on to Sarah. She took it out of the box, this she'd definitely keep. She was about to put the clothes back in when she noticed something else in the box. It was a red handkerchief and it reminded her of the one she'd read about in the diary. The one that Frank had given to her nanna with the letter from her grandad sewn into the hem. Perhaps it was the same.

It was used to wrap something up. It was a piece of cloth with a 'C' embroidered on it. A pink C surrounded by little yellow flowers. Sarah held it out in front of her. It was a bib. A pretty, homemade baby's bib. It must have been Camille's. Sarah thought it odd that the only thing that was kept from when her mum was a baby was a bib that wasn't even hers. Sarah traced the C with her fingers and wondered what had happened to the little girl that once wore it. The more Sarah looked for answers, the more questions she found. She was pretty sure Camille was the key to all this and finding out what happened to her might tell Sarah everything she wanted to know.

Sarah picked up the handkerchief and looked at the edges. One of the hems was loose and showed signs of being stitched and opened up again several times. Goosebumps popped up all over her arms as she realised this was indeed the same piece of cloth that had transported notes from her granddad's hiding place back to her nanna. But where were the letters? Had she not kept them? Was it too dangerous to keep notes from a husband on the run? Maybe she'd burned them after reading. What Sarah wouldn't give to read those little notes of love and hope? With great care, as if she was handling an ancient artefact, she wrapped the bib up in the handkerchief and put it back in the box with the baby blanket. Everything else she put in the pile of things to get rid of. It was a strange feeling deciding which of her mum's possessions were worth holding onto and which ones weren't. Especially as her mum kept so little already, the very few things she did must have meant a great deal to her.

After the discovery of the bib and the handkerchief in the attic that morning, Sarah was even more determined to find out what happened to Camille. She phoned Alice who had worked for the city of Amsterdam ever since she left college. She promised to send Sarah some links to the online archive so she could search for them in the birth registers and gave her the phone number of a retired historian whom she knew would be happy to help Sarah.

"Don't get your hopes up though, Sarah," Alice said. "We don't have a lot of information to go on."

"I know, I know. But I need to try. I have a feeling there's something strange going on and I don't know what it is."

"Like what?"

"I don't know," Sarah said slowly shaking her head. "Something just feels odd."

"I found Camille's bib in the loft," she said after a pause.

"That's nice. I'm not sure it's strange though. You should see the stuff my mum has kept from when I was a baby. Maybe your nanna wanted something to remember her by."

"But there was nothing of my mum's. No clothes, no cuddly toys, nothing. Only Camille's bib. The loft was empty apart from one little box and it had nothing of my mum in it."

"Okay, that is a bit weird."

***

"What would you like to know Sarah?" asked Yvonne.

"I'm not really sure to be honest." Sarah told her about the diary and that she wanted to find out what happened to Clara and Camille. Yvonne, the retired historian Alice had told Sarah about, had invited her to come over for a coffee and a chat.

"There is a lot of documentation from that time. The Nazis were meticulous when it came to keeping records. They wrote down everything; who was deported, who lived, who died." Sarah heard the "but" before it was said.

"But there is also a lot that wasn't recorded. Like Jewish births. Most Jewish babies, especially the ones born after 1943, weren't registered until after the war. It was just too dangerous to document their little lives."

"That makes sense," Sarah said. "Clara was already in hiding when she had Camille so I guess she'd not have had a choice in the matter."

"That's right, it would have been far too much of a risk for both Clara and the people hiding her."

Sarah wondered how this would affect her search.

"There's also another thing to keep in mind," Yvonne's tone changed, became darker. "Many of the babies who didn't survive, don't have their lives recorded at all." Yvonne gave Sarah a bit of time to digest this. "For some there wasn't anyone left alive to do the registration, birth or death. Many families were completely wiped out. From those who survived, a lot of parents found the loss too painful to deal with, especially if they had lost more than one child. Formally registering the deaths was too much for some. They'd been through so much, the only way they could continue after the war was to start afresh by burying the memories so deep, they'd never come to the surface again. And maybe in time they'd forget themselves."

Sarah hadn't considered this before, she'd assumed there'd be a record somewhere, she'd just have to find it. It made sense though, after all, Paul had tried to deal with Emma's death in a similar way.

"So even if Camille survived, if Clara didn't, there might still not be a record for her?"

"That's right." Sarah's earlier optimism started to crumble.

"That would make it impossible to find her."

"I'm sorry, Sarah, I know this is not what you wanted to hear. It doesn't mean you won't be able to find her, but it's important to know why Camille might not be in any archives." Sarah nodded, it was a bit of a blow but at least she was more prepared for what she might or might not find.

"If there is anything else I can help with, please do give me a ring. I hope you find Camille."

Me too, Sarah thought.

Yvonne had agreed with Sarah that it'd be best to focus on looking for Camille. Clara had been such a common name at that time and without knowing her surname or date of birth, it'd be impossible to find her. Camille was a far more unusual name and even though she didn't know the exact date of birth, she knew roughly how old she was when they arrived at her nanna's house. Earlier, Alice had emailed her the links to the parts of the online archive where Sarah was most likely to find her. As soon as she got back home, Sarah sat down at her mum's desk to start her search. She was also armed with a list of sites to check that Yvonne had recommended. Records of known hiding places, forums with information on survivors and endless lists of unlucky souls, who never came back home from the camps.

First, she searched the online birth register for her own name and date of birth just to see what she could expect to find. It was pretty straightforward if you had enough information for the person you were looking for. Excited and nervous, she typed in Camille and the birth year of 1944 and hit search. Sarah closed her eyes for a few seconds waiting for the website to return its results. She wasn't expecting many hits but she was surprised when it was only one. It wasn't what she hoped. The only name that came back was Camiel and even though the birth year was correct, the record stated he was a boy. She changed the birth year a few times, just in case an error was made or someone else had registered her after the war and got the date wrong but there was nothing. A search for Clara brought back far too many results and as she was unable to narrow it down by birth date it was no use.

Desperate to find anything, even if it was bad news, Sarah started trawling through pages of people who never made it back from the concentration camps. There were so many records to check and so many places to search. She looked through list after list until her eyes hurt and she felt like she was going around in circles. Seeing all those names made her realise it was likely that Clara and Camille never saw the end of the war. The number of deaths was incomprehensible. All those children who had known nothing other than hunger, cold and cruelty in their short lives. The names started to swim in front of her eyes and she couldn't go on any longer, she needed a break. To clear her head a bit she went for a walk. Her mum had always believed strongly in the therapeutic power of a bit of fresh air and exercise in the same way the British immediately start making tea in a crisis. And, as always, it worked. She came back feeling refreshed and ready to start again. To take a break from the lists of casualties, Sarah looked through some of the forums where people looked for the fates of friends or relatives. Sarah was surprised by the number of people who, still after all this time, didn't know what had happened to their loved ones or the people who'd been instrumental in the escape or the hiding of now-deceased parents or other family members. She looked through some of them to see if she could find any mention of a Clara or Camille. She found a few Claras but none that could be hers. Reluctantly, she went back to the heartbreaking task of looking for them amongst the victims. She didn't want to read all the names and ages but, also, she couldn't look away. The sound of her phone ringing snapped her out of her daze. Sarah looked up and saw it flashing on the table, apart from the monitor Sarah had been staring at, it was the only other light in the room, she hadn't noticed it had gotten dark.

"Have you found them yet?" Alice asked.

"No, I looked everywhere but there isn't a sign of Camille anywhere. It's like she never even existed."

"That sucks! What about Clara?"

"I found lots of Claras but unless I find a way to narrow down the results there are just too many to check out." Sarah tried to swallow the lump that was blocking her throat.

"Are you okay?"

"Yeah, I'm fine," she said not really believing it herself. "Just a bit down."

"Why don't you text Jack?" Sarah could almost hear the cheeky grin that she envisaged was spreading across her friend's face. "I'm sure he can cheer you up."

"Maybe."

"Go on, send him a message. You know you want to. And chin up, we've only just started looking. These things take time."

Sarah knew Alice was right, it had only been a day and, so far, they'd just looked in the obvious places, who knew what they'd find if they'd delve a bit deeper. She was also right about Jack, hearing from him would cheer her up. She wondered what Paul would think. Would he be jealous? Relieved she was moving on? Or perhaps he'd not even care.

Sarah's mind felt like a ball-pit with 20 toddlers jumping around in it. All those hours of searching without finding even a trace of what she was looking for had left her overwhelmed and exhausted. She was done for the day.

After a long shower she texted Paul to ask how he was. Then she sent another message:

Hey, fancy an ice cream?

***

"I miss her, Em, I miss your mum."

Emma's grave at the top of the hill, from where she could see the duck pond and the playground, had become Paul's quiet place. Ever since Sarah left for Amsterdam, to give him the space he thought he needed,

113

he'd started visiting his daughter's resting place every day during his lunch break. The time on his own had been more than enough to allow his heart to, first, fully break for the second time, in order to let the pain in and then, bit by bit, begin to heal. Before, he only visited on Emma's birthday and even then, only because Sarah insisted he'd come. His denial, in the end, got him nowhere.

Chatting to her every day made it all real, painful but real. Sometimes he imagined Emma as the three-year-old she'd now be, giving him her blunt toddler wisdom and more often than not he knew she was right. Today she asked him the very simple question "Why don't you ask her, daddy?" Paul looked at his imaginary daughter and smiled.

"Ask mummy to come home."

Chapter Nineteen

Amsterdam, February 1945

Louise wrapped her scarf around her head and cuddled Anna close in an attempt to keep them both warm. The wind felt like rough sandpaper rubbing her cheeks and the sleet made it treacherous to walk. She was worried about taking Anna out in such cold weather but she didn't dare leave her with Clara again, not after what happened last time. Frank might be one of the good guys but that didn't mean there wasn't anyone else ready to question and report on her actions.

Luckily, she'd got out early that morning and the queues weren't too long yet. It took her less than an hour to get to the front of the queue. After lunch, she'd go out with her extra ration coupons. It was too suspicious queuing for food with a bag that already looked to have a day's worth of rations in it so she would make two trips, hoping there'd still be some food left.

"Let me help you with that, Louise," Frank said walking up behind her.

"Oh Frank, you made me jump." Louise laughed nervously. "You have a real skill sneaking up on people." She briefly touched Frank's arm and gave him a smile. She hoped it looked as genuine as she meant it.

Frank just nodded and took her bag off her even though it wasn't at all heavy. There wasn't enough food to fill up a shopping bag, let alone make it hard to carry. They walked in silence. The only things Louise wanted to say to him couldn't be said out here in the street. When they got to her door, she turned to face him, looked him straight in the eye and asked if he wanted to come in for a drink.

"I don't have any coffee but I can heat up some water."

"Water will be fine Louise and who likes the taste of coffee anyway," Frank said with a wink.

"Yes, who needs coffee." Louise said without being able to keep the longing from her voice. Before the war, she wouldn't do anything in the morning until she'd have a strong and sweet cup of coffee in her hand. How she missed that bittersweet flavour.

"I'm sorry, Frank," Louise said busying herself with the stove. She kept her head down not wanting to look up.

"For what?"

Louise sat down but still didn't look him in the eye.

"For thinking you were a traitor." Finally, she looked at him and was surprised by the kindness in his eyes. "When you saw me without Anna the other day I got scared."

"Don't worry, Louise, you don't have to apologise. A lot of people think I work for the Germans. Ironic really." He smiled the saddest smile Louise had ever seen. "It's fine, honestly. It's actually safer this way. People stay out of my business because they're scared I will betray their neighbours or their friends, so I can get on with things undisturbed." They sat in silence for a few minutes, both lost in their own thoughts.

"Thanks for the letter from Peter. It's such a relief to know he is alive. Have you seen him?"

"No, I haven't but I know he is in a very good hiding place. One of the best. I could try and get a letter to him if you'd like to write one? I can't guarantee anything but if you sew it in the handkerchief, I will do my best."

"That would be wonderful, Frank, thank you so much."

"Just don't write anything that could identify either of you in case it is intercepted."

"Of course," Louise said. "How do I get it to you?"

"Don't worry about that, just keep it with you when you go out and I'll make sure I will get it off you."

They chatted about the weather and the meagre rations for a while and Louise told him about the soldiers that turned up on her doorstep earlier that week.

"What do I do Frank?"

"Pray. Pray that they don't come true to their promise or that they're too busy trying to win this war which, thank God, is looking less likely every day."

Frank's answer didn't put Louise's mind at rest but it was nice to at least share her fears with someone.

"Keep your chin up, girl," Frank said as she walked him to the door. "It might all be over soon."

As soon as Frank had left Louise sat down to write to Peter. She kept the tone light as there was no point him worrying about her. He had enough on his mind.

My dearest,

All is well. Your little girl is as good as gold. Keep strong. You are in our   thoughts all day and all night.

Sending you all our love.

Louise rolled the note up as tight as she could and sewed it into the hem of the handkerchief. She folded it up, kissed it and put it in her coat pocket, ready to take out with her tomorrow.

Chapter Twenty

The taxi dropped Sarah off a couple of minutes' walk away from the restaurant. She needed a bit of time to calm her nerves before she went in. She was, in theory, still a married woman and she couldn't help feeling guilty for arranging to meet another man for dinner. Especially someone she'd only met once. And someone for whom she'd spend ages deciding what to wear. After having all her clothes out on the bed earlier that afternoon, she'd taken Alice's advice and went for her denim mini-skirt, a fitted grey jumper, black leggings and her brown leather boots. She was happy with the result, it showed she made an effort but didn't look too keen. Just before her taxi arrived, Paul had phoned and even though she still had no idea where they were heading and how he felt about it all, it had been nice to talk to him. They carefully skirted around the subject of when, or if, Sarah would come back home. At some point they'd have to talk about it but for now neither was ready for that yet. She was sure though that going back to the way things were was not an option. Paul had sounded relaxed and, even though she could hear the sadness in his voice, she could tell he was more positive than he had been for a long time.

As soon as Jack saw her, his eyes lit up. He took Sarah's coat and pulled out her chair for her. A bottle of champagne was on the table and he poured her a glass.

"To a lovely evening," Sarah said as she held up her glass.

"To you," Jack replied. Her body's reaction to his cheeky grin confirmed what she already suspected. She was in trouble. It had been a long time since she last fell in love, but not so long that she didn't remember how it started. The bubbles tickled Sarah's nose when she took a sip. She was grateful for the glass to keep her hands from fidgeting. Jack leaned over to brush a lock of hair out of her face. It sent a sparkling current through Sarah's body.

"We'd better order some food before this champagne goes straight to my head," Sarah said.

"Good plan, I'm starving. What do you recommend?"

Sarah pointed out some dishes that she liked and they both ordered the fillet steak with mushroom sauce and fried potatoes.

"So, what brings you to Amsterdam?" she asked.

"Believe me, you don't want to know."

"Ah, but I do," Sarah said with a smile.

"Would you believe me if I said I wanted to smoke some weed?"

"Nope, you're not the type."

"Are you saying I'm boring?" Jack said with a pretend offended look on his face.

"Not at all. But if you go to high school in the middle of Amsterdam and you spend many free periods in and around coffee shops, you soon learn to recognise who does and doesn't smoke."

"Yes, I guess you would." Jack said.

"Did you? You know, smoke?"

"Not really," Sarah said scrunching up her nose. "I tried it a few times but I didn't like it. It stinks."

Sarah looked Jack in the eye. She was still waiting for him to answer her question.

"So, you really want to know my boring reason for coming to Amsterdam?" Sarah nodded.

Jack squinted his eyes and a big smile crawled all over his face.

"Nope, I'm not going to tell you." Even though she enjoyed the banter, hiding his reasons for being here flared up her old insecurities as quickly as her heart rate. Did he really like her or did he accept her invitation out of pity? "I'm having too much fun to let it all get ruined by talking about my problems." Sarah relaxed a little, at least, he said he was having fun.

"Okay, I'll let you off for now. But at least tell me how long are you staying for?"

"I go back tomorrow."

"Oh," Sarah said unable to hide the disappointment in her voice.

"But let's not think about that. Let's enjoy our dinner and make the most of the time we have."

"Wow, are you always that positive?" Jack laughed.

"Definitely not. Most of the time I'm pretty miserable really." Sarah doubted this was true. So far he'd been the perfect company. Charming, although his refusal to answer any question seriously was a bit suspicious. He made her laugh though. She couldn't remember when Paul had last done the same. She feared the last time they had any fun together had been before Emma died. Three years without laughter...

"So, out of the three simple questions I asked, you only managed to answer one seriously. At this rate it is going to take a long time to get to know you, Jack Rodgers."

"That's what I'm counting on." Jack took a sip of his champagne and as he put his glass down he brushed Sarah's hand with his thumb leaving a tingling trail on her skin.

"So how about this husband of yours?" Sarah laughed out loud. She liked his charming way of changing the subject although it wasn't one she was keen on discussing.

"Still working through stuff, I think." she said thinking of a way to steer the conversation in a different direction.

"I'd say I'm sorry but I'd be lying. I think it's great news that he is stupid enough to let you go to Amsterdam on your own meeting handsome fellas like me." Jack's wink made a little ball of fire bounce around in her stomach. She liked him. Far more than she should. His twinkling eyes, his handsome face and that smile. She could look at his smile all night.

"Do you have kids?"

The question took Sarah by surprise and the smile that had been solidly set on her face since she walked into the restaurant disappeared instantly.

"I do. I did...I...." Sarah drained her glass and stared out of the window. Every time someone asked her this, seemingly innocent, question she felt like she jumped off a bridge rushing towards the water, bracing for impact. Normally she did quite a decent job of hiding the feeling but when it came as unexpected as it did now, her coping mechanisms didn't have time to kick in. She didn't want to talk about this, she wanted to laugh and forget about all the pain for a while.

Jack poured her another glass and Sarah gratefully took a big gulp.

"I don't want to talk about it. I'm sorry."

"No need. I understand." Jack reached out over the table and took Sarah's hand.

For the first time since they met, the silence they sat in had become uncomfortable.

"I'll tell you something else though," Sarah said pleased to have thought of a subject to lighten the mood. She told Jack about the diary.

"Wow, that's pretty cool," Jack said, also clearly relieved that the conversation was going in a different direction.

"It is. Neither my nanna or mum ever talked about the war and all I ever knew was that my granddad died a couple of months before liberation."

"Do you know why they never talked about it? My grandad was a pilot in the war and he talked about it all the time, we had trouble getting him to stop going on about it. I remember one story where his navigation equipment failed and he got lost. He only just made it back to England before his fuel ran out. He must have told us that at least a hundred times."

"No idea, they just dodged the subject whenever it came up."

"That must have been tough on you, growing up without knowing what happened during that time."

"It was. I know nothing of my mum's life before she met my dad. It's almost as if she didn't exist until then."

"I guess it wouldn't be easy reliving all the horrible things that they must have seen and lived through. Often we cope with suffering by trying to forget what happened and avoiding the subject."

"I think you're right and I get that now," Sarah said as their food arrived. "But I really struggled with it when I was younger. Not knowing anything about my Mum's childhood was hard and I always felt left out, like they were keeping secrets from me or they thought I wasn't old enough to cope with it. I know now that was probably just the mind of a suspicious teenager but what I really don't get, even now, is why nobody told me about Clara and Camille. Risking your own life and that of your baby to save someone else is such an amazing and brave thing to do. Why would you keep that a secret?"

"I don't know. I can't imagine what it must have been like to live in a country at war. Constantly fearing for your life and that of your loved ones. And then risking your own to save a complete stranger? You come from brave stock, Sarah."

"I don't feel very brave." Jack took her hand and gave it a little squeeze.

"Did Clara and Camille survive the war?"

"That's the thing. I don't know. The diary stops suddenly a couple of months before Amsterdam was liberated and I have no idea what happened after. I've been trying to find out by looking for Camille, but with only first names to go by, I'm not sure if I'll ever be able to find out what happened for definite and whether they made it. I wish my mum had told me about it."

"Maybe she didn't know. Maybe she had only recently read the diary herself."

"Maybe." It was an option that Sarah hadn't yet considered. She'd assumed that her mum had always known and chosen not to tell Sarah but given the silence surrounding the past, it was certainly possible that she'd been as much in the dark as Sarah.

"I'm really sorry about your mum, I wish there was something I could do to help."

"You're already doing it." This time it was Sarah who took Jack's hand. She wanted to say or do something to show him how much she liked him but for some reason she held back. Was it guilt? Or was there still a fragment of hope that her marriage could perhaps be saved?

"Do you know what I find hardest about losing her?" Sarah said as she finished her drink and moved the last few bits of her dinner around her plate. "There's nobody left in the world who loves me unconditionally. Without question. You know the way only a parent can. That feeling that, no matter what you've done or what happened, there is someone there to catch you. She was always there for me, Jack, always. And now it's just me. I have nobody left."

"You have me," Jack said. Sarah leaned forward a little, the need to be close to him was getting stronger by the second.

"It must be really hard losing a parent you really loved." Jack said.

"Are your parents still alive?"

"No, they died years ago. I didn't love them all that much and I doubt they really cared about me and my brother." Jack said with a shrug of his shoulders.

"I'm sure that's not true."

"Unfortunately, it is. They ran their own company and both worked at least 80 hours a week. We were pretty much raised by au-pairs and shipped off to boarding school as soon as we were old enough."

Sarah's childhood couldn't have been more different. Even though her mum always worked hard to provide for them both, Sarah never felt she wasn't around when she needed her.

"I've made my peace with it though. They weren't bad people, I just think they weren't cut out to be parents. When they died, I used the money they left me to buy my house and start up my own business. I'd never been able to do that otherwise."

Sarah loved the way he turned a horrible situation into something positive rather than spending his life hating his parents for what they did or didn't do. "Never hold a grudge," her mum always said. "The only person who suffers from a grudge is the person holding it." Jack was the living proof that her mum had been right about that. Maybe one day he could teach her how to do it.

"Anyway, do you want some dessert?" Jack asked. "Ice cream perhaps?"

Sarah laughed.

"No, thanks, but I quite fancy a walk if you're up for it?"

"I love Amsterdam in winter. The worse the weather, the more beautiful it looks to me." Sarah said as they left the restaurant.

"Now that's something you don't often read in the tourist brochures; Amsterdam - even better when it rains."

Sarah felt her hand brush Jack's, she didn't pull away, even though she felt she probably should. He took her hand and folded his fingers into hers. The internal debate between "you're still a married woman" and "he wanted this break" was impossible to call. They were both right. Sarah knew that allowing this to go further would only lead to more complications in her already tricky love life. Maybe she should let go of his hand, thank him for a nice evening and say goodbye. It would certainly keep things simpler. But she didn't. She held onto him and as he gently stroked her knuckles with the tip of his fingers. A warm glow slowly spread through her entire body. They walked in silence for a while, still holding hands and stealing glances at each other when they thought the other wasn't looking.

"She died," Sarah said so quietly Jack could barely hear her. Her voice thick with pain.

"An infection. She was four months old." The lights of the city turned star-shaped through Sarah's eyes.

On a small bridge over one of the canals they stopped and Sarah stared into the water. Jack didn't say a word but Sarah could feel his kind eyes on her which gave her the strength to tell him more. "There was nothing they could do to save her. She died in my arms."

Jack kissed Sarah's hand and wiped a tear from her cheek. She liked how he didn't say anything. How he didn't try to find the right words to make her feel better because he knew he couldn't. Nothing could ever make it better. Nothing could bring her back.

"What was her name?" He asked quietly.

"Emma." Sarah tried her hardest to keep away from the dark hole that was getting closer and closer. She couldn't go back in. She had to stay in the light. There. With Jack.

It started to rain but neither of them made a move to leave.

"You're going to happy again, Sarah. I know you can never get over a loss like you've suffered but you're an amazing woman and you deserve to be happy. I want you to be happy." Sarah leaned into him and for a moment she forgot about the loss, the pain and her broken marriage. All she wanted was his arms around her to make her feel safe and let her believe that maybe, one day, she could be happy again. That maybe there was a life for her after Emma. After Paul. And against all better judgement, she let him kiss her.

"Are you okay?" Jack asked as they were getting close to the house. Sarah had been quiet ever since they left the bridge.

"I think so. Life is just a bit complicated at the moment."

"I guess I'm not helping with that."

"No, you're most definitely not." She squeezed his hand. It was refreshing to be able to talk honestly without the constant fear of rocking the boat.

"Why don't people have curtains in this city?" Jack asked as he peered into the houses they walked past.

"What?"

"Nobody has curtains. You can just look straight into kitchens, living rooms, why don't people have curtains?"

"I don't know. I've never really noticed to be honest. Maybe it's a war thing." Jack looked confused.

"I mean, maybe after such a long time of forced black out, all people wanted was to be able to see into the world without restrictions."

"Could be, people must have felt so cut off from the rest of the world, especially people living on their own. I guess that was part of the reason behind it."

"This is me," Sarah said as they reached the house. She rummaged in her bag for her keys. She felt Jack stepping closer but kept her eyes on her bag, the keys already in her hand. Jack gently lifted up her face and stroked the back of her neck. No matter how hard she tried, she couldn't keep away from him, she wrapped her arms around his waist and pulled him against her. "Make it more complicated," she whispered in his ear.

"Okay, Mrs Fisher, if you say so." With twinkly eyes and strong arms Jack pushed Sarah against the door and kissed her. When he let her go, her legs wobbled.

"Do you want to… Do you want to come inside?"

"I do, but I should go and pack." Sarah's shoulders slumped and she went back to looking for her keys blinking repeatedly. Jack kissed the top of her head.

"Thank you for a lovely evening."

"Will I see you again?" she asked.

Jack pinned her back against the door and kissed her again. Deeper and with an urgency that made Sarah feel like her whole body was melting.

"You bet, Mrs Fisher. Real soon, I hope," he whispered in her ear and walked away without looking back.

Chapter Twenty-One

Amsterdam, February 1945

The handkerchief with the letter to Peter safely hidden in a, now, neatly stitched hem, was tucked into Louise's coat pocket. She'd been carrying it around for days hoping to walk into Frank but she hadn't seen him. She was worried he might have forgotten about it as he probably had more important things on his mind than dropping off letters from worried wives. But hearing from Peter had been such a relief and being able to let him know they were well was giving her so much hope.

The queue was inching forward which normally meant that food was running out. There wasn't enough food for everybody. The people of her beloved city were starving all around her. Even with the extra ration coupons her parents had given her, it was still a daily struggle to feed both her and Clara. How she'd have coped without the extra food, she didn't know. The hunger had started to make her feel weak and dizzy and the queues were so long it was hard standing up for all that time. She'd nearly passed out whilst waiting the day before. She'd given most of her breakfast to Clara who needed it more than she did as she was not only feeding Camille but also Anna when Louise couldn't satisfy her. Luckily, Mrs van Dijk was in front of her and kept hold of her until it passed, otherwise she'd have lost her place in the queue.

It wasn't just people's stomachs that suffered from the hunger, their compassion and humanity were taking a hit as well. Mrs van Dijk told her that last week an old lady had collapsed while queueing for food and at least 10 people just stepped over her to take her place. Finally, someone helped her up, probably forgoing their own food for the day by doing so. The war brought out the worst in some people, while others stepped up to be heroes. Louise knew that whatever she was challenged to do, she'd rather die than having to live with herself knowing she could have helped someone but had chosen not to.

"Morning." Louise jumped.

"Oh, Frank, how do you do that? You always spook me, I never hear you coming."

"Just trying to keep you on your toes."

They both laughed. It was these little talks that made the day bearable for Louise. At home, she only had Anna to talk to and sometimes she craved adult conversation even more than food. She was surprised by how much she missed simple human interaction. Everyone had become so scared of trusting the wrong person that most people stopped talking to anyone apart from their very closest friends and family.

"How is little Anna doing?" Frank asked.

"She's fine, thank you." Louise put her hand in her pocket to make sure the handkerchief was still there. She couldn't remember whether they'd agreed anything for the handover. Then Frank sneezed loudly and, with his hand still over his mouth, he gave her a look. Louise quickly pulled the handkerchief out of her pocket and handed it to him.

"Here you go, Frank," she said, feeling silly for worrying. Frank was working for the resistance, of course a simple letter handover wasn't a challenge for him.

"Thank you, Louise." Frank wiped his nose and put the handkerchief in his pocket. "I'll wash that for you. You should have it back within a week or so."

"Thank you." Louise tried to keep her tone light but she couldn't stop her voice from quivering. She'd hear from Peter again soon. All of a sudden, the long day she had ahead of her didn't seem so daunting.

Chapter Twenty-Two

Sarah couldn't help but smile. The corners of her mouth kept curling as if they had nowhere else to go but up. The only thing that stopped the grin from spreading all over her face was the awful job of going through her mum's wardrobe. She'd delayed it for long enough now. For days she set the intention only to find an excuse to not do it. The decisions on what to keep, sell or throw away laid heavy in her stomach. The desire to just keep everything was strong but Sarah knew that she had to move on. She thought of Emma's nursery at home, still exactly the way she left it when she took Emma to hospital. A constant reminder of what happened. Not allowing them to move forward. Despite the loneliness flooding over her every time she put another outfit on the bed, she kept going. Then her mind drifted back to Jack and she allowed the smile to cover up the tears. They'd had a wonderful evening. At first, she'd been disappointed that Jack hadn't accepted her invitation to come in but after she had some time to think, she liked the fact that it hadn't turned into a meaningless one-night-stand. Maybe this meant there was a possibility it could turn into something more. Did she want more? She thought she did but where did that leave her marriage? She could imagine Alice's answer to that question: "Exactly where it is now, nowhere." And she'd be right. To her surprise she'd still not missed Paul for a second. She was sad that things had gone so badly wrong and she felt lonely most of the time but she didn't miss him. Surely that said enough about the state of their relationship. Even if she hadn't met Jack, her and Paul were probably beyond repair.

Her phone bleeped with a message from Alice.

"Can we meet for lunch please?" Sarah replied that she'd love to and they arranged to meet at a café near Alice's work. She couldn't wait to tell her about the night before.

The prospect of lunch with Alice killed the last bit of motivation Sarah had left for sorting through her mum's clothes. It was still only 11 am but she quite fancied a bit of shopping and left for town early. She hopped on a tram and thought about her nanna and how she'd have coped in the war without any public transport. She'd have had to walk everywhere. That must have only added to her isolation and the strain she'd already be feeling having to deal with the secret of Clara and Camille all on her own. It put Sarah's loneliness into some perspective. At least she had the freedom to go wherever she wanted. She also didn't live in constant fear for her life nor was she cold or hungry.

Sarah had an hour until lunch and she wandered in and out of several shops without paying too much attention to the wares they had on offer. After everything that had happened in the last couple of months, it was nice to wander around without a goal or a destination. When she was about to walk out of one of the clothes shops she used to like as a teenager, but that now sold nothing she'd even consider wearing, she heard a familiar voice. She turned around and caught the eyes that had caused her to smile all morning but now made her heart drop.

"Sarah?"

"Jack?" There were lines on his face that hadn't been there last night and his eyes shifted from Sarah to the young girl standing next to him.

"Are you coming, Jack?" A woman who looked like she'd stepped right out of a fashion magazine, grabbed his hand and started pulling him away but he didn't move. The woman turned to Sarah and looked at her with a mix of curiosity and annoyance.

"Jack?" The woman said as she claimed possession of him by putting her hand in his back pocket.

"Sorry," Jack said. "Sarah, this is Debby, she is -"

"His wife," Debby interrupted. Jack looked at her through squinted eyes. His jaws clenched together as if they were physically holding back his anger.

"Debby, this is Sarah." It was hard not to notice the tenderness in his voice when he said her name. Debby threw him a look that made it clear she'd heard it. Sarah, however, hadn't. All she could think was that he'd lied to her. He was meant to be travelling home, not go shopping with a wife and daughter she didn't even know he had. She felt the pressure of tears at the back of her eyes.

"I have to go," she said as she ran out of the shop.

***

"The bastard!"

"The bastard!" Sarah and Alice said in unison before they'd even sat down.

"You first," Sarah said.

Alice fired off a list of obscenities to describe her landlord who was going to kick her and Linda out of the house they'd rented for the last five years.

"There's no way we'll ever find anything anywhere near as nice in the city centre. Not anything we can afford anyway. And he's only giving us 2 weeks to move out! Bastard!"

Alice loved the centre of Amsterdam, the buzz of the city ran through her blood and Sarah couldn't imagine her ever living anywhere else.

"Can he do that? Surely he needs to give you more time?"

"He can do whatever he wants. We don't have a contract. We knew it was a bad idea at the time but the house was so perfect that we took it anyway. It looks like we're about to pay for that mistake."

Sarah felt bad for her friend who was always the first to offer help to anyone who needed it. She didn't deserve this.

"I'm sorry, I wish I could help. I can go and give him a piece of my mind? Scare him into letting you stay?" Alice nearly choked on her burger.

"You? No offence but how exactly would you scare a 6ft5 man? Poke him with your violin bow?" They both laughed but Sarah did want to help her friend and she was racking her brain to think how.

Maybe there was a way for Sarah to use the situation she was in to both their advantage. Sarah waited for

Alice blow off some steam. She knew in that state, she would not be open to any suggestions, good or bad. When she stopped ranting to have a drink Sarah jumped in with the idea that had been forming in her head.

"Why don't you move into my mum's house?"

"What?"

"Why don't you rent my mum's house off of me? I know it's not as central as what you have now and you'll have to share with me for a while until I sort myself out, but you can move in whenever you want. We can decorate my mum's room for you and Linda can have my old room as her office."

"Are you serious?"

"Of course."

"But I thought you were going to sell it?"

"I was, but that was before Paul decided he needed a break. Now I'm not sure I even want to sell it. It's the only place where I feel at home. And, for now, I don't actually have anywhere else to go."

"Are you sure you won't mind sharing with us?"

"Not at all, it'll be fun! And you'd be helping me out as well. If I have a bit of money coming in each month I won't have to rely so heavily on my savings. So you'd be doing me a favour really. And you'd get mates' rates of course," Sarah said with a wink. She knew that Alice's calm look was just a front that hid most of her emotions. Over the years she'd learnt to recognise the tiny changes in her friend's appearance that betrayed her feelings. Shoulders raised slightly higher than normal, less eye contact, and the ever-telling change in her tone of voice. All three signs were present and Sarah smiled.

"It would be awesome, thank you so much. I'll ask Linda this evening but I know she'll be dead pleased."

Sarah felt a bit better for helping Alice who had been the one jumping on a flight at a moment's notice to help Sarah deal with Emma's death. The first year without Emma she must have travelled to England at least once a month. First to help Sarah through the most difficult days like Mother's Day, Emma's first birthday and Christmas. Then later on she'd take Sarah out to the pub for a drink or to go dancing even though Sarah did everything she could to convince Alice she didn't want to go.

"I know," Alice had said. "But we're going anyway."

And when they did, Sarah found that she started smiling again and sometimes she even enjoyed herself. Alice made her feel alive again. To finally be able to do something back felt good.

"Your turn. Who pissed you off?"

Sarah told her about her first about her date with Jack last night and then the run-in with him earlier.

"There might be a perfectly reasonable explanation?"

"Maybe. I'm not sure I want to hear it though."

"Why not? I thought you liked him?"

"I do. But not only did he lie about going home this morning, he also never mentioned this small detail about being married and having a daughter."

"Yes, there is that," Alice said in the cool tone she used when she was about to slap out some truths, whether Sarah wanted to hear them or not.

"I say phone him, invite him over, let him explain and have fun making up. Not all marriages are the result of true undying love, I'm sure you're aware of that, some can be pretty fucked up and maybe he didn't want to tell someone who he'd just met that he stupidly married someone he shouldn't have." Sarah didn't look convinced.

"Look, you don't have to marry the guy but please allow yourself to have a bit of fun."

"I'll think about it," Sarah said but, even though she knew Alice was probably right, she wasn't at all sure she would follow her advice this time. She'd had enough pain to deal with recently. She didn't need any more.

On her way home Sarah passed the shop where she bought the flowers for her mum's funeral. She went in to say hello to the owner who had known her mum well. Growing up there'd always been fresh flowers on the dining table and they'd always come from there. Walking in, the smell of all the different blooms tickled Sarah's nose and brought back memories of coming with her mum, early Saturday mornings, to buy a bunch or two. She inhaled deeply and looked around at the abundance of flowers, even though it was only early March. As she scanned the shop, a small olive tree caught her eye. It was hiding amongst some potted house plants and looked perfect to plant in the garden as a memorial for Emma.

"That's a wonderful thing to do, Sarah. Your mum would have loved that."

"I think so too."

"Here, have these hyacinths on me to maybe plant around it. She loved the smell of them."

"Thank you, that's very kind of you."

It was these little gestures that made Sarah realise how many lives her mum had touched. It was comforting to know she'd been so loved.

Even though it was only a small tree, carrying it home was awkward. The branches kept poking her in the face and the leaves tickled her nose. Her arms were aching and she could barely see where she was going. Every now and then she'd put the pot down and rubbed her hands together, she should've worn gloves. Her thoughts drifted back to this morning when that familiar voice had made her heart skip a beat only for it to be crushed seconds later. She wondered why he had lied to her when she'd been honest and told him all about her marriage.

When she was nearly home, even with her vision impaired by shoots of olive wood, she recognised the figure getting up as soon as he noticed her. Her hands became clammy and the tree nearly slipped from her grip.

"Let me take that for you," Jack said reaching out for the pot. Sarah turned to move it out of his reach.

"I can manage, thanks," she snapped. Awkwardly holding the pot with one arm she got her key out of her bag and open the door.

"I'm sorry, Sarah, please can I…" She didn't give him the opportunity to finish his sentence and shut the door in his face. Inside she kicked off her shoes, put the tree by the back door and sat on the sofa with her coat still on trying to ignore Jack's knocking on the door. She got her phone out of her bag to text Alice and was greeted by a long list of calls and texts from Jack asking if she'd please let him explain.

"Explain what? That you lied to me? No thanks."

She dropped the phone on the sofa and stomped to the kitchen to make a cup of tea. Even in her anger, the temptation to check her phone for his reply was almost too much to resist. She needed a distraction and time to think.

Upstairs she ran herself a bath. A hot soak was the perfect way to get her mind of him. Hopefully he'd soon get the message that she wasn't planning to let him in and leave. When she stepped into the warm water and let herself be enveloped by bubbles she could no longer hear knocking. He must have gone back his hotel.

"Good riddance," she said out loud although deep down she could detect a tiny slither of disappointment.

When her skin had become wrinkly and the water had gone cold, Sarah felt calm enough to get out and check her phone. There were several messages from Jack, all asking if she would just let him explain. But it was the last one that caught Sarah's eye.

"She's not mine, Sarah. Meghan is not my daughter."

Not telling her about having a child was what had upset Sarah the most. Of course she was pissed off that he'd not told her about being married but Alice was right in that he may well have had a good reason for hiding it. Some marriages were just stupid mistakes that should never have happened but a child was different. Marriages could be regretted, not children. But if that girl wasn't his daughter, maybe the situation wasn't quite as unforgivable as she'd initially thought. Another message. "She's not mine, please, can we talk?"

It was as if he knew that the girl was the key and Sarah was ready to hear his side of the story.

"Please."

"Ok," Sarah replied. "We can meet for a coffee tomorrow." She might have been ready to talk but she had no intention of making him think she was desperate to hear his explanation. He could wait.

"That's great. Any chance we could talk now? It's getting quite nippy out here."

"Wait, what?!" Sarah threw her phone back onto the sofa and rushed to open the front door. Jack jumped up off the step and looked at her with drooping eyes. He rubbed his hands together in an attempt to warm them up. Sarah couldn't help but feel sorry for him. The sadness seemed to be pouring out of him. She stepped aside just enough to give him space to squeeze past. She tried to ignore his hand briefly resting on her hips but found she couldn't.

"Tea?" Sarah offered.

"Yes, please."

"You must be freezing. Why aren't you wearing a coat?"

"I wasn't expecting a three-hour stint outside when I left for a quick shopping trip this morning." He looked at her with eyes that almost melted her heart but she wasn't ready to give in just like that.

"I just wanted to explain." Jack said when she handed him a cup of tea.

"Okay, shall we start with the wife you somehow forgot to mention? I know I shouldn't really talk as I'm married myself, but at least I told you about it. And who's the girl? And why did you both look so stressed?"

"Debby is my ex-wife. I met her 5 years ago and we got married three months later. We couldn't have been a worse match. I was a fool. Completely dazzled by her looks and over the moon that someone like her could want me. I'm not proud of it but I just wanted her to be mine."

"Sounds like a fairytale," Sarah made no attempt to hide her sarcasm. Even if he wasn't as guilty as she'd initially thought, he'd still hidden his marriage from her. He deserved to feel ashamed.

"Like I said, I'm not proud of it. And we're not together anymore. The divorce came through a couple of weeks ago."

"It sure didn't look like that to me. And anyway, last night you told me you were going home this morning." The accusing look in Sarah's eyes was hard to miss.

"I was but I changed my ticket." When he showed no sign of offering further explanation as to why he'd changed his travel arrangements, Sarah walked to the kitchen to give herself a couple of minutes to think. She could feel his eyes on her back.

"Nobody knows what Debby is really like," Jack said when she sat back down.

"She puts on this front and everyone just loves her. My friends and family all think she's great but all they see is this gorgeous woman putting on a show. They have no idea what she's actually like. How she manipulates everything and everybody including her own child. How she goes off with her friends and just leaves Meghan to fend for herself and how she punishes her if I don't dance to her tune."

"Maybe you should tell them?"

"Maybe." The man Sarah saw in front of her showed no resemblance to the one she kissed last night. This Jack looked beaten, fragile even.

"Is Meghan the reason that you're here?"

"Yes," Jack said. He looked ashamed but Sarah no longer wanted him to. She'd jumped to conclusions and now regretted her harsh reaction. She sat down next to

143

him and put her hand on his leg. She started to understand why he hadn't told her.

"I'm sorry, Jack. When I saw you this afternoon, I thought you were playing me. I shouldn't have jumped to conclusions."

"You have nothing to be sorry for. I should have told you but it's not really a story I enjoy telling." Jack fiddled with his cup of tea. "Especially not to someone I'd like to impress."

Sarah smiled but he wasn't quite out of the woods yet.

"Why didn't you go back this morning?"

"When I came back to the hotel last night, I was so happy. I enjoyed spending time with you and I wanted more. So I changed my ticket to the end of the week. I was hoping to surprise you tonight." A smile started to travel across Jack's face but it didn't get a chance to light up his eyes as his face darkened again.

"Meghan had been upset about me leaving today so I texted her this morning to let her know I was staying a few more days and when she told me Debby had kept her home from school to go shopping, I went to see them to try and talk sense into her, I mean she can't keep Meghan home from school for stuff like that, but she wouldn't listen, so I went with them." Jack looked down at his cup of tea. "I know she's using me but I'm struggling to find a way out without leaving Meghan to deal with all of this on her own, she's only 9."

"Maybe you should talk to someone. Someone who can look at the situation objectively and help you come to a solution that works for everybody. You clearly care a lot about Meghan and you can still be part of her life but without putting your own on hold."

"You're right, maybe the best way to help both of them is to get an outsider involved. I know she's not my kid and not my responsibility but I want to do right by her."

"She's lucky to have you," Sarah said as she moved in to kiss him.

Chapter Twenty-Three

Amsterdam, February 1945

Every day since those awful soldiers threatened her to give up her love "or else…", Louise had prayed and hoped Peter was safe and well. She hadn't had a reply to her letter yet and the longer it took, the more she worried. There was no way of knowing what they'd do to him if they found him or to her if they didn't. She was left to imagine the worst.

It had been exactly a week ago and from the moment she got up, she'd tried to convince herself that maybe they'd forgotten. But she couldn't even pretend to believe it. And at 3pm, they knocked on her door again, banging so hard it made her cup shake on the table. Only one cup this time, Clara had not been downstairs that day.

Louise rushed to open the door and recognised the angry one, she'd never forget his face, but the other two were new. The one at the back, broad and very tall, was holding someone.

"Mama? What's going on?" Louise said when she realised it was her own mother being dragged into her hallway. Louise begged the soldier to please let go of her.

The angry one nodded almost unnoticeably and the soldier released her. Louise threw herself into her mother's arms.

"Are you all right? Did they hurt you?"

"I am fine, my dear." She took her daughter's face in her hands. "But they have your father."

"What? Why have they got Pappa?"

Louise's mother stroked her cheek.

"Oh darling, I'm so sorry." She took a handkerchief with a lace edge that had once been white, from her sleeve, dapped her own eyes and then Louise's.

"What has Pappa done? Why do they have him?" A long silence followed. Too long for the angry soldier.

"Tell her!" he barked.

She took a deep breath and with a tremble in her voice she told Louise.

"He's done nothing, my sweetheart, nothing." She wiped her eyes again. "But they won't let him go until we tell them where Peter is."

"But I don't know where Peter is!" Louise said with a high-pitched voice. "How can I tell them something I don't know?"

"I know and it's all right. Everything will be fine." Louise desperately wanted to believe her but deep in her heart she knew nothing would ever be all right again.

"We will kill him at midnight if you do not tell us where your husband is." Louise sharply sucked in a shivering breath. Without another word, the soldiers turned on their heavy heels and marched out of the front door. Her mother swayed on her feet and Louise grabbed hold of her. She would not let these monsters see her weakness.

"What are we going to do?" Louise asked when the soldiers had left.

"Nothing, my sweetheart, there is nothing we can do."

"But we need to get him out! We can't just leave him there. I know someone I can ask, he will tell us where Peter is. He got a letter from him to me. He knows where he is."

"Frank won't tell you, my love. He knows Peter is too valuable to the resistance to give him up."

"You know Frank? How do you know Frank?"

"Everyone who's fighting knows Frank, my dear."

"Fighting? What do you mean?" Louise's mother gently led her to the sofa and sat her down.

"Your father has been working with Frank from the start."

"Pappa is in the resistance?"

"Yes. We didn't tell you because we didn't want to put you at risk, it's better not to know too much. The Germans don't know either, otherwise they would have killed him already."

Louise stormed out of the back room and got her coat.

"Where are you going?"

"I'm going to see Frank, he'll know how to get dad out." Her mother grabbed her hand and gently but firmly pulled her away from the door.

"You can't," she said.

"Why not? I'm sure Frank would help."

"You can't because if they're watching, and they probably are, you'll lead them straight to him. We need Frank. We need him to do what he does." Louise's shoulders slumped. "If they arrest Frank, hundreds of people will be in danger." Louise slowly took her coat off.

"But what about Pappa?"

"Your father would not want to risk other people's lives to save his own." Louise knew she was right. He'd always been brave. His office job didn't suggest it but Louise knew. He was her hero.

***

When she was five years old her father had taken her for a walk along a river during their summer holiday. He'd always loved water.

"If I ever get rich," he said "I'll buy us a boat."

"And I'll be captain."

"Yes, Captain Louise. And we'll sail around the world chasing pirates and fishing for food."

"And make sun hats from sea weed," Louise giggled.

Their fantasy world disappeared instantly when they walked over a bridge and heard a splash followed by a piercing scream. A little boy had fallen into the water. His parents were on their knees trying to grab the boy's hand but they couldn't reach him and he went under. His mother let out another scream. Without a second of thought, Louise's father took his shoes off, told her to stand still and hold on to the bridge until he came back and he jumped into the water.

"Don't let go of the bridge!" he shouted as he swam to where the little boy had disappeared below the water. He dived down and a few seconds later he came up with the boy in his arms. He was coughing and crying. But he was alive. Her father swam him to shore and, after handing the boy to his mother, he climbed out himself. The boy's father shook his hand and when he took his wallet out of his pocket, Louise saw her dad shake his head. He rustled the little boy's hair and went back to where Louise was still holding on to the bridge, just as she was told.

"Good girl," he said. He put his shoes on and they walked back to their holiday cottage, leaving behind a trail of water. She knew then that whatever happened, her father would always be there to save her.

***

It was this memory of her father that helped her through the endless hours that followed. Louise desperately wanted to go and beg the Commandant to spare her father but her mother wouldn't let her.

"These people are evil, they don't have a compassionate bone in their bodies. You know Mrs Suurbeek from around the corner?" Louise nodded. "Her husband was arrested for stealing ration tickets. They were going to kill him for it. She went down to the station to plead for his life but instead she was forced to watch him be executed and then they killed her too."

"That's horrible but we can't just sit here and wait for them to kill him?"

"We can and we will," her mother said in a calm voice. How she remained so composed, Louise had no idea.

"We will pray for his brave soul," she continued. "It's what he would have wanted. He'd never forgive me if I put your life or my own in danger to save him." Louise embraced her. "Why don't you make us a drink and we will pray for him together." Her voice sounded hoarse now and her eyes were wet. Louise did as she was told. The two women sat at the table with an untouched cup of warm water waiting for time to pass. At some point they made some dinner together and Louise wasn't even surprised when her mother, without saying a word, dished up three plates and gave one to Louise to take up to Clara. How she knew, Louise did not know or ask.

Together they put Anna to bed in her little basket downstairs. Louise couldn't bear to not have her nearby.

After Anna had her late-night feed, Louise handed her to her mother who held her as she watched the hands of the clock move towards midnight and then past it. Silent tears ran down her cheeks as she cuddled her granddaughter a bit tighter and held her as close as she could.

The next morning, she went home to wait to be told of her husband's death. Louise offered to go with her but she said she wanted to be alone. Watching her from the doorway, she was no longer the strong woman Louise remembered. She walked with her head hanging down low, looking inches shorter than before, and didn't turn around to wave. She just walked. Slowly.

When Anna fell asleep later that morning, Louise got the chair from her bedroom and opened the loft hatch.

She climbed up the ladder and sat down next to Clara who was feeding Camille. She had no words to tell Clara what had happened. She had only tears.

Chapter Twenty-Four

With a cup of freshly brewed coffee Sarah sat down on the sofa inhaling the bitter scent and enjoying a moment of quiet. So much had happened over the last few days that she was looking forward to a day on her own with nothing to do or worry about. Sipping the hot liquid, memories of the night before turned the corners of her mouth up. She'd not wanted him to go this morning but he'd promised to take Meghan to school and the last thing Sarah wanted was to make their, already complicated, relationship any harder, so, reluctantly, she'd kissed him goodbye hoping they'd meet up again soon.

As she looked out into the garden she saw the sun peek over the fence and light up a little spot of ground right next to her mum's favourite bench. It looked like the perfect place for Emma's olive tree, catching the very first sunlight even in winter. Also, it was one of the few places in the garden where nothing was growing.

Still in her pyjamas, Sarah moved the pot out into the patch of sunlight and got the shed key from the kitchen. The shed was as tidy and organised as the house. All the tools were clean and hanging in a row on their own hooks. Lots of pots were stacked up in the corner ordered by size and the sun lounger was leaning against the only clear wall. Sarah smiled. Her mum's neat ways had always calmed her when she felt stressed. She remembered in her last year of high school, she was studying for her final exams and she'd gotten so worried about her history exam, she'd thrown her book down the stairs and spent the next 20 minutes stomping around the house slamming doors. Initially her mum had let her get on with it, knowing that an angry teenager was best left alone until the rage subsided. Then, she'd come up with a cup of hot chocolate, a plate of biscuits and the history book. She sat on the bed and didn't say a word until Sarah had finished her drink and was nibbling on a biscuit.

"Let's tidy that desk of yours," she'd said. "Surely you can't think straight with so much chaos around you." Sarah had frowned at her in the way that only teenagers can and hadn't moved off the bed. Whilst her mum tidied up, Sarah told her what the exam was about and by the time her desk was clear, so was her head. She spent the following two hours studying and nailed the exam. Her history score turned out to be the highest out of her entire school.

Sarah took a trowel from its hook, kneeled next to the bench and started digging. As soon as she put the trowel in the ground she shivered. It felt like a cold hand was running up her back. When she took the trowel out of the ground it stopped. With every scoop of earth she took the shivers got worse. It felt like the soil objected to being disturbed. She tried to shake it off but the deeper she dug, the stronger it became. Sarah wondered whether there was a reason nothing was growing here. Did her mum have the same experience when she tried to plant something? Sarah shook her head and, cursing her foolishness, she kept digging. As soon as the tree was in and she'd patted down the soil, the feeling was gone. In its place she felt warmth flooding through her body as if the ground was relieved it was, again, left in peace.

Sarah was pleased with the spot for Emma and sitting next to the little tree made her feel calm and safe. In their house, in England, she felt restless and unsure of herself. She couldn't remember whether it had always been like that or if it started after Emma had died.

She wasn't an overly confident person, apart from when she picked up her violin. As soon as she started playing, she felt like no challenge was too big and she could conquer the world with her music. She loved performing, both solo and as part of the orchestra she'd been playing in ever since her student exchange days. The music would pulse through her body and change her into a different person. Someone who didn't worry what anyone thought and who was perfectly content with herself and the moment. All that changed when they lost Emma. The passion she used to play with faded and the pleasure of performing disappeared altogether. She was paralysed by nerves every time she walked onto the stage and in the end, she had no other option but to hand in her notice. Teaching had been the logical next step and even though it didn't give her the same rush the sound of applause used to, she enjoyed getting the best out of her students and prepping them for the career she'd had to give up. She knew she'd done the right thing but no longer being able to do what she loved and what she worked so hard for did get her down. All Paul had ever said was that she should do what she felt was right. But this kind of support wasn't enough for Sarah to gather the courage to get back on the stage. Sometimes she wondered whether she'd have been strong enough to get back to performing if Paul had pushed her a bit. Instead she started feeling more and more unsettled and lonely, unaware of his pain as he didn't communicate this until it was, perhaps, too late. But there, in the house that had been in her family for so long, she felt grounded. Like her roots were still there even though her mum no longer was. Maybe this could be her home again. Maybe she should stay.

Feeling stronger than she had in years, she phoned Paul. The moment she realised that it was in Amsterdam she felt at home, she knew they had to talk. After weeks of wondering what he wanted and what she herself needed it was time to discuss their future. If there was one.

"Hey, it's me," Sarah said as Paul answered after only one ring.

"Hi, you're alright?"

"Yes, thanks. Sorry for ringing you at work."

"That's okay, I was going to phone you this evening actually." Sarah was relieved he sounded cheerful, she didn't really want to bring up the subject of their marriage if he was in a bad mood.

"Is everything okay?" she asked.

"Yes, I'm just working some things out and I think we should sell the house."

The subject of the house and whether they should move had been hanging over them ever since a friend had asked them a year ago if they had any plans to sell up and move. Deep down they both knew they needed to but neither was ready to let go of the house that was still full of Emma. Paul had answered that the market wasn't in a good place for them to sell and Sarah had been relieved the real reason for not moving had been effectively avoided. That night she woke up to find Paul missing from the bed. She knew he'd be in Emma's room.

It was dark, the only light came from the pink nightlight that still came on every evening at 6 o'clock because neither of them had wanted to switch it off permanently. She watched him for a couple of minutes just sitting there, his head hanging down but she didn't disturb him and went back to bed. When she got up three hours later, after not being able to get back to sleep, he was still there. At 6am, the night light switched off and Paul got up to get ready for work. He never said a word about that night and they never discussed moving house again. She wondered what had changed? Even though Paul had erased every sign of Emma from their living areas and bedroom, the nursery was kept exactly as it was. He wouldn't allow anyone other than him and Sarah to go in and nothing could be moved, changed or gotten rid of. Everything was kept exactly as it was when she was still alive.

"Are you sure?" She asked.

"I think so. I don't think we can move on while living here. I'm ready to make a fresh start. Maybe we can have look at some houses when you come back?"

157

"Sarah?" Paul said when she didn't answer for a long time.

"I'm not sure I want to come back, Paul." It was only when he'd mentioned buying another house together that Sarah knew she didn't want that.

"But what about us?"

"I've met someone," Sarah said as an answer to his question.

"Oh," Sarah shut her eyes and rubbed her forehead. It was obvious that Paul hadn't been expecting this outcome. And neither had Sarah. But now it was out in the open it felt like the right thing to do.

"Is it serious?" Paul asked.

"I don't know, but I really like him."

"Are you happy?"

"No," said Sarah after a pause. "But I feel like I could be again."

"In Amsterdam?"

"Maybe, I don't know. It feels good to be here."

"Then maybe you should stay."

To take her mind off the conversation she just had with Paul, Sarah flicked through her nanna's diary scanning the pages without really reading the words. She still couldn't quite believe all that happened in the house she grew up in without her knowing about any of it. Suddenly a name on one of the final pages stood out to her.

Frank.

Wasn't there a Frank in her mum's address book? Didn't she send him one of the cards notifying him of her mum's death? She'd spent hours writing names and addresses of all her mum's friends on the thick, cream coloured envelopes. It was a strangely therapeutic process. She hadn't really paid attention to what she was writing, she just copied name after name, address after address. But she was pretty sure there'd been a Frank. She got the address book and flicked through it with nerves rushing through her body. If he was in here and if it was the same Frank, he might know what happened to Camille. He could even know where she was.

"I knew it!" Sarah said as she found it.

Frank van Nes - Siem

Sarah looked at it for a while and wondered whether Siem was maybe a nickname? There was both an address and a phone number. She dialled the number before she had time to worry about what to say. The lady who answered the phone introduced herself as Marijke.

"Hello, I'm looking for Frank. Frank van Nes?"

Chapter Twenty-Five

Amsterdam, February 1945

At first Louise wasn't sure what had woken her up. Was it the cold? Given the lack of feeling in her feet that were sticking from under the blanket, it was certainly possible.

Then she heard a sound, coming from downstairs, that made the hairs on the back of her neck stand up. Last time she heard it, her life changed dramatically. For a moment she considered pretending not to have heard it, she didn't need any more complications in her life, but she knew she'd never be able to ignore someone in need of help.

Lighting the way with her dynamo torch, she got to the back door and lifted the curtain a little. It was Frank. Louise let out a relieved sigh. Then she saw someone was with him, a man she'd never seen before. He was leaning into Frank as if he was unable to stand on his own feet.

The urgent look in Frank's eyes made her open the door as quickly as she could. The two men shuffled in, the unfamiliar man leaning heavily on Frank, and Louise shut the door and drew the curtain.

"I'm sorry, Louise, I had no choice but to come here," Frank said.

"Not a problem," Louise said, speaking not entirely truthful. "Let's sit your friend down in the back room."

Louise settled him on a chair and, with a creepy feeling of history repeating itself, she put her coat on his shivering shoulders. Frank was still in the kitchen, she found him leaning against the worktop. He had black circles under his eyes and his eyebrows were folded into a frown.

"There was a raid," Frank said looking as if he was talking to nobody in particular. "We'd known for a few days we'd probably have to find a new hiding place for Joseph, that's his name, but when we got to the address we arranged for him, the Germans were all over it, dragging out the whole family, the children, everyone. The children were hanging on their mother's skirts but the soldiers grabbed them by their hair and pulled until their little hands had to let go. Their screams went straight through me. I can still hear them now." Frank stood there, staring into space, shaking his head.

When Louise put a hand on his arm, he finally looked her in the eye.

"I'm sorry, I don't want to involve you but you were the only person I trust who lived near enough. Joseph isn't well, he can't walk far."

161

"It's fine, Frank. I'm happy to help." Louise said, not feeling the confidence she was trying to convey.

"Thank you. I'll pick him up again first thing in the morning. I just need a few hours to find him a place."

It looked to Louise like he needed some sleep more than anything else.

"Have him ready before sunrise." Frank said as he stepped out of the back door.

"Stay safe, Frank."

Frank nodded and disappeared into the night.

Upstairs, Louise helped Joseph into her bed and sat down on her chair to rest. Joseph tossed and turned and talked in his sleep. Nothing Louise could understand but it sounded anxious.

When the clock downstairs chimed for 5am, Louise lit the stove with one of her last books, she'd have to keep the final ones for emergencies, and warmed up her own breakfast for Joseph. Clara would have the rest, she herself could do without today.

Just as Joseph finished the last of his soup, she heard the tapping noise again. Quickly opening the door, she let Frank in.

"It seems one night here and you look a different man," Frank said to Joseph who had joined them in the kitchen, looking indeed a little brighter than he had last night. A weak smile slowly appeared on his face. Louise hoped he'd have a safe place to go to.

"Thank you," Joseph said as he took her hands.

Frank was silent. His expression seemed to say both "thank you" and "sorry".

Chapter Twenty-Six

"She's met someone," Paul said to himself in the car on the way to work. "She's met someone." The many beers he drank last night, that failed to soften the impact of those words, still sat heavy in his head. His eyes, hidden by dark sunglasses, stung a little. He hadn't meant the harsh words he'd said to Sarah in a failed attempt to make it hurt less. It hadn't worked and he'd apologise later.

How much easier would it be if he hated her? If he didn't want her back so desperately it ripped his heart in half every time he saw her empty side of the bed, or her tea cup standing idle in the cupboard. He'd lost both his girls and he had no idea what to do next.

***

Marijke van Nes looked a lot younger than Sarah had expected. She was well dressed and didn't show any signs of the age she probably was.

"Please, have a seat," she said "Would you like a coffee?"

"Yes, please," Sarah said as she sat down. She was unsure of how to start the conversation not knowing how Marijke felt about the past. She needn't have worried, Marijke brought it up herself.

"I moved in here after, Frank, my father, passed away. It was his house. I have no brothers or sisters and my parents loved this house so much I couldn't bear to sell it."

Sarah smiled, recognising the sentiment. On the phone, she'd told Marijke about her search for Camille and she was pretty sure that the Frank described in the diary was indeed her late father.

"It's been a long time since anyone has asked about my father and the war," she said with a kind smile.

"Thank you so much for seeing me," Sarah said. "Neither my mum nor nanna ever talked about the war, so anything you can tell me would be very helpful."

"It's my pleasure, Sarah, it's good to know that your generation has not forgotten the trials of that time. There are many stories that should be told and remembered. And I think I have something you'll find very interesting."

Marijke handed her a tiny notebook, only a little bigger than a credit card. The spine had worn thin and it looked in danger of falling apart from the lightest touch.

"Go on, open it," she encouraged her with a nod of her head.

"For the ones I couldn't save." It said in tiny but very neat writing on the first page.

"It's my father's ledger. He started it shortly after the end of the war and in it he recorded the fate of all the people he tried to save. I haven't looked through it in years but I thought your Camille might be in it."

Sarah looked through the first few pages. Each had one or more names written at the top followed by details of hiding places. Some were marked as survived and others confirmed as dead. Most had mentions of previous employment, rough age or a pre-war address. Sarah felt a rush of excitement every time she turned a page. The next entry could be Clara and Camille. Would there be an address for them? Or something else that could help Sarah find Camille?

"He used to carry it in the breast pocket of his shirt. 'Close to my heart, like all the people in it,' he always said."

Sarah carefully looked through the ledger. There were so many names in it. Did Frank really save this many people?

"Every time he found out what had happened to someone he tried to help, he'd update his little book. Every confirmed survivor meant a celebration at home, but if he had to add a date of death, it would send him into a spiral of depression."

Sarah didn't know what to say. It was obvious that Frank had saved, or at least tried to save, so many people but she also understood how heavy the weight of all those deaths must have been for him.

"He was never able to accept that he did all he could," Marijke continued. "On bad days when he found out about several deaths he would whisper 'What if I'd done more? What if I'd done more?' over and over again."

"That's so sad."

"It wasn't all bad though. In the spring of 1947 he married Esther, my mother. She was a young Jewish woman he had helped escape to a safe place. She'd been in hiding just around the corner from here and Frank kept in touch with the family who hid her. He saw them regularly and one day he was there when Esther popped round for a coffee. They fell in love there and then, although I suspect my father had feelings for her a long time before that and was hoping he'd bump into her there." Marijke showed her a framed picture of Frank and Esther on their wedding day. Esther's smile filled up most of her face and Frank's happy grin was even wider.

"This photo was taken just after Frank told her that they'd met during the war."

"She didn't know?" Sarah asked. "She didn't know he saved her life?"

"No, Frank didn't tell her until they had given their vows. He didn't want her to marry him because she thought she owed him."

"But how come she didn't recognise him?"

"I asked her that same question once. I thought that if someone saved your life, you'd surely be so grateful that you'd never forget their face." Marijke's face turned more serious. "It was dangerous to know people, she told me. It was a risk to even walk around with your head held high. Especially for Jews. Hiding and avoiding eye-contact, constantly trying not to stand out had become second nature. She remembered the day Frank took her to the place where she stayed until the end of the war. She remembers every second of the walk along

166

the canals. The fear of running into soldiers and the relief when they locked her in the damp cellar where she would live until liberation, two long years later. But what she didn't remember was who had taken her there. She didn't remember Frank."

Marijke took the photo from Sarah, put her hand over the image as if to bless the people on it, and put it back in its place.

"They lived a good life. They both had their demons but they were happy."

"I'm glad he was happy," Sarah said. "From what I read in my nanna's diary, Frank was a good friend to her in those difficult last few months of the war."

"I'm pleased to hear that and I know Frank would be too. Have a look through the ledger. I hope it will be of help."

Gently Sarah turned page after page of the fragile notebook until one of the entries made her breath catch in her throat.

Clara (diamond polisher) and Camille (baby)
Hidden by Louise - Jan & Greta's daughter
Escaped - unconfirmed

"They're in here! Clara and Camille are in here!" Marijke rushed to her side and Sarah showed her the entry.

"So they escaped from what I assume was your nanna's house, but it looks like Frank never found out what happened to them after that."

Sarah was excited to have found mention of them but, at the same time, disappointed she still didn't know whether they survived or not.

"I imagine it was very difficult to track people down in that time?" Sarah asked.

"It really was. Most Jewish people had lost their homes. They were either taken by the Germans who often gave them to Dutch people who were working for them, or people who needed a house just grabbed their chance and moved in. When the surviving Jews started returning, months after liberation, a shameful part of Dutch history began. Some squatters, because that's what they were really, were decent enough to move out when the rightful owners returned but others turned them away at the door. After surviving not only the concentration camp but also the death march back home, some walked for months to get back from Germany, they found themselves without a place to live. It still shocks me how awful the Jews were treated even after the war had ended." Marijke paused for a few seconds. "So even if Frank knew where they lived before they went in hiding, that didn't mean he could find them afterwards." She looked at Sarah who couldn't keep her eyes off the page in Frank's ledger. It was the only proof, other than the diary, of Clara and Camille actually existing.

"It has diamond polisher in brackets after Clara's name," Sarah said. "I assume that was her job?"

"Most likely, yes. Frank tried to write down as much as he could remember to make it easier to find them. He obviously didn't succeed, but maybe it will help you find Camille."

"Maybe. Frank was clearly very thorough, he must have spent a lot of time on it."

"He did. A while after he married my mother, she begged him to stop looking for survivors. There was so much more bad news than good and it was getting him down. She was worried about the effect it had on him."

"And did he stop?"

"He did." Marijke smiled. "He still carried the book with him and he updated it when news found him but he no longer looked for it. It wasn't until I was a teenager that he was ready to put it away. He went through all the names and wrote unconfirmed where he wasn't sure what happened. Then he locked it away and never looked at it again."

"He sounds like an incredible man," Sarah said.

"He was. Far more than he ever realised or was willing to accept." Sarah shut the ledger and held it up but Marijke didn't take it.

"You keep that, it might help you in your search."

"Are you sure?"

"Sure. Frank would have wanted you to have it. Just promise me one thing. When you find out what happened to Clara and Camille, please update it."

Sarah promised she would and then she asked Marijke if the name Siem meant anything to her.

"Sure, that was Frank's code name in the resistance. Not many people knew that though."

"It was in my mum's address book."

"He must have thought your mum a close friend if he told her that. Even after the war, he didn't often mention his time in the resistance."

"I wish I'd have met him."

"He would have liked you," Marijke said as Sarah put her coat on to leave. "Good luck with the search."

"Thank you," Sarah said. "For everything."

Chapter Twenty-Seven

Amsterdam, February 1945

"I'm not sure you should go," Clara said as she handed Louise her coat.

"I have to, it's as cold in the house as it is outside now. We need to warm up the girls, I'm worried about their health."

"Please don't take Anna though, it's too cold and dangerous." Clara pleaded. She could see the doubt in Louise's eyes. "Leave her here, she'll be better off in her own bed than out in the cold night."

Louise didn't say anything but handed Anna to Clara.

"Don't worry about us. And stay safe."

"I'll do my best."

Louise had not been out after curfew before. The complete darkness was overwhelming and disorienting. She stood still keeping hold of the doorpost for a minute, letting her eyes get used to the dark. She shivered, the cold was bad enough during the day but now, without the little bit of sun they got every now and then, it was even worse. Keeping her breath shallow, breathing in too deep felt like cold knives slashing her throat, Louise slowly moved away from the safety of her front door. Taking careful steps, she moved slowly.

In the city's parks, the cold people of Amsterdam had started chopping down trees to heat their houses. But you needed more strength for that than Louise had left. It was also far too dangerous. The police no longer warned before shooting. She'd overheard someone in the queue for the soup kitchen mention the little blocks of wood that could be found in the tram rails. They could be dug up and were the perfect size for the stoves many now used for heat and cooking. It was still dangerous but if she was lucky the darkness would be enough to hide her actions.

It took only a few minutes to get to the closest tram stop, there wasn't anyone around but Louise was too worried about being seen with houses on either side of the track. She walked alongside it for about 20 minutes until she came to a bit where the track veered away from the road. Just as she was about to crouch down and look for the blocks she'd come for, she saw a shape move towards her on the track.

"Move away! This is my patch," hissed the dark figure.

Louise jumped back and quickly walked on moving away from the track in a wide circle to pass him. She looked back and saw it was only a boy, he was so small and far too young to be out by himself at this hour.

When she was far enough away from him, she knelt down and looked at the track.

There were a few of the little blocks left but she couldn't get them out. Her hands were too cold and the blocks were dug in too deep. She walked a bit further and when she saw one that was sticking out a bit, she used the kitchen knife that she'd brought both for protection, you never knew who'd be out and about at this time, and to help get the wood out from the track. It was hard work digging and prying the frozen soil and several times her hands slipped down the knife, almost cutting her fingers. It took her ages, hours it seemed, to get the first one out. The next two were a little easier as she now knew how deep to dig, but her legs were getting stiff and she didn't think she'd be able to get many more before her legs ached so much she might not make it back home. Just as she glanced back at the boy, worried he might be moving too close in her direction, she heard something approaching, it sounded like a bicycle. All of a sudden there was a beam of light showing the boy hunched on the tracks. Louise jumped off the track and ran for cover. She assumed the boy had done the same. He hadn't. He seemed oblivious to the light at first and when he did look up it was already too late. Three gunshots cracked through the quiet night and the boy slumped down over the tracks. Louise carefully looked around the lamppost, that she hoped would keep her from suffering the same fate as the boy, and saw the police officer responsible for the shot pull the boy off the track and dumped him not far from where Louise was hiding. As if nothing happened, he got back on his bicycle and rode off.

After a couple of minutes waiting, trying to steady her heartbeat, Louise slowly walked towards the boy, looking left and right, praying the policeman wouldn't appear again. When she reached the boy there was no need to check whether he was still alive. His eyes were open and stiff with fear. Louise kneeled down next to him, said a quick prayer and got up to go back home. The few blocks she managed to dig up would have to be enough. After a few steps she stopped; turned around and walked back to the boy. Without looking into his glazed eyes she pried the cloth bag containing the wood he'd collected out of his clenched fists.

"God forgive me, but you won't be needing these anymore."

The next morning, the stove, which was now burning the wood Louise had dug up from the tracks, radiated a special kind of heat. A heat that not only warmed them up from the outside but that burned deep in the pit of Louise's stomach. The heat of not giving up, of fighting, would keep her warm long after the flames had gone out.

Chapter Twenty-Eight

Sarah couldn't stop staring at the entry in Frank's ledger. The very little information it contained made a huge difference to her search. It filled her with hope and gave her new energy to keep looking. If they had escaped, they might have survived? Maybe they had to leave Amsterdam? Maybe that's why Frank couldn't find them and why there wasn't a mention of them in the archives. They could have built their lives elsewhere. It seemed a perfectly possible scenario. Still, it bugged Sarah that if that was what had happened, why would Clara not have gotten in touch with her nanna after the war ended? The awful times they shared must have created a strong bond, one that, you'd think, would last a lifetime. She would have expected them to be friends, or to stay in touch at least. That is, if she survived. The ledger might not have answered whether they lived to see liberation day or not but it did give Sarah a snapshot of Clara's life before the war. She worked as a diamond polisher. It didn't say where, but at least it was a starting point.

Sarah felt more positive now she had a lead to explore. She could investigate the diamond factories to see if they had any records of Clara. She'd never taken an interest in them before, it was one of those things that mainly tourists did, but perhaps it wouldn't be such a bad idea to have a look around. It wasn't like she had much else to do. Jack had gone back to England for a job he promised to do a while back and she missed him more than she thought she would. They spoke on the phone often and he'd promised to come back to visit her soon. When she told him about her and Paul breaking up, he offered to jump on a plane that same day.

"Don't you have a job to finish?" Sarah asked, smiling at his enthusiasm.

"Oh yes, of course. But I'll come as soon as I'm done."

Sarah couldn't wait to see him again, especially now she'd no longer feel guilty for seeing him behind Paul's back.

"How's England? Miss you xx"

She didn't need to wait long for Jack to reply that England was cold and wet and that he missed her too. Sarah couldn't help but wonder if they could have a future together if she decided to stay in Amsterdam.

***

"This is amazing, Sarah, thank you so much for letting me have a look at it," Yvonne said as she held the ledger as gently as you would a newborn baby. Sarah had asked her for more help now she had a new lead on Clara.

"You're welcome. It's exciting to finally see some sort of confirmation of what my nanna described in the diary. Not that I didn't trust her word," Sarah added quickly. "But another source telling the same story makes it just that little bit more real. Does that make sense?"

"It does, I totally understand what you mean."

Sarah gave Yvonne a minute to look through the ledger.

"Do you think I have more of a chance of finding her now I know what she did for a living?" Yvonne smiled at her in the same way her mum sometimes did when she knew Sarah was throwing herself into something without taking time to think things through.

"I don't know but I'd be happy to help you try and I know exactly where to start."

Chapter Twenty-Nine

Amsterdam, February 1945

"Thanks for the bread, Frank, you didn't have to but it's appreciated nonetheless."

"You deserve it, Louise, we're all very grateful for you helping out with Joseph. We need his skills to keep things running, we'd struggle to do all we do without him. When we found him a safe hiding place, the first thing he said to me was to make sure we'd give you something to show our gratitude. I'm sorry it took so long."

Louise waved his apology away.

"Would you like a slice, Frank?"

"No, no, you enjoy it, I have to go."

As he opened the door to leave, Louise grabbed him by the arm and pulled him back in.

"I want to do more."

Frank quickly shut the door. Louise had been thinking about it ever since her father was killed. Sitting at home doing nothing but wait for the war to end was no longer an option. She was too angry. She needed to do more.

"You're already doing enough. Peter would never forgive me if I put you into more danger."

"Peter isn't here and I am more than capable of looking after myself."

"I know that, but are you sure you want to take more risks?"

"I am. I want to fight."

Frank sighed with a pained look on his face and gave her an address to meet him at the next morning.

***

"The soup kitchen?" Clara asked when Louise brought up her breakfast and a jug of water, her eyes lit up when she saw the small piece of bread. Louise had resisted the temptation to eat it all in one go and had only had a small piece herself and wrapped the rest back up for tomorrow. As soon as Louise handed the plate to Clara, she brought her face close to the plate and breathed in deeply through her nose as if smelling it was as good as tasting it. With difficulty, she put it to one side to eat it later.

"What does he want you to do in a soup kitchen?"

"I don't know. Maybe he wants me to help cook? He didn't seem too keen to put me in more danger so maybe this is his way of giving me something safe to do that will still help."

"I hope so. Do you want me to look after Anna?"

"No, he specifically told me to bring her. Not sure why."

***

The soup kitchen was housed in an old restaurant that closed early on in the war. What happened to the Jewish owners, Louise didn't know but she hoped they were safe. As she approached, she saw a side door ajar and judging by the sounds and smells emerging from it, it was safe to assume this was the actual kitchen. She parked the pram out of sight and picked Anna up who had been asleep most of the way. She stirred but after a stroke on her back and some soothing words she fell back asleep on Louise's shoulder.

"Can I help you?" A woman sweating over a huge steaming pan asked.

"I'm not sure, Frank told me to come."

"Down the stairs, he's expecting you," she said, pointing in the direction of a door without taking her eyes off the pan.

Behind the door weren't the stairs Louise was expecting. Instead she stepped into a larder with a ceiling that sloped down the further you walked into it and very little food on the shelves. Louise walked back into the kitchen. "This is a cupboard?" She asked.

"Keep walking, just mind your head and shut the door behind you."

Louise did and let her eyes get used to the dark. With her hand up over her head on the sloping ceiling, she felt her way forward. The further she got in the cupboard, the more she had to duck. Until, just as she thought she'd have to get on her hands and knees, the ceiling suddenly lifted and she could stand upright again.

In front of her was a door and, as there was nowhere else to go, Louise opened it. It creaked and she hesitated before going through. Holding Anna tight, she stepped into a room lit only by a couple of candles. Frank was talking to someone who was leaning against a stack of crates. Louise couldn't see what was in them. She cleared her throat and Frank turned around.

"Morning, Louise, thanks for coming," he said easy as if she'd come to join them for a cup of coffee, but Louise heard not a word of what he'd said. All her senses were fixed on the man standing next to Frank. He was wearing an army uniform. Louise stared at the eagle, above the man's breast pocket, holding the swastika in its claws. She held onto the doorpost to steady herself.

Why was Frank talking to a German soldier? Was this a trap?

"Frank, what is going on?"

"Don't worry, Louise, he's on our side," Frank answered.

The soldier stepped forward holding out his hand. "At your country's service, madam."

Louise couldn't bring herself to shake his hand but she nodded her head, holding Anna even tighter.

"This is Olaf, he's been helping us for a couple of years now. You can trust him."

"If you say so, Frank."

Frank rummaged in the crates behind him and held up a package. "We're in need of couriers to transport anything from ID cards to small weapons or the odd wireless."

"A courier? Me?"

"Yes," Olaf continued. "Women, especially those with babies, are the least risky. Most soldiers don't expect a mother with a baby to do such a thing. They very rarely get caught,"

"But sometimes they do," Frank interrupted. "If you do get caught, they'll almost certainly execute you, baby or not."

"I'm in," Louise said. Now holding her hand out for Olaf to shake, which he did.

'If you're sure, Louise," Frank said.

"I am."

Frank nodded and rummaged through the crates. He handed Louise something that looked like a fabric envelope. The top was soft as a pillow and underneath was a flap that opened up a space to presumably hide the delivery. Next he gave her a parcel of similar size to the fabric envelope. She slid the parcel in and used the two buttons underneath to do it up.

"Use that as a pillow in Anna's pram, it won't look suspicious if you get stopped. You're only in trouble when they search the pram."

Louise thought back to the day exactly that had happened and she wondered whether the enemy was far more aware of their tactics than the resistance knew. It didn't stop her wanting to help though. Doing nothing and letting other people take the risks was no longer an option for Louise. She wanted, she needed to fight. Even if it killed her.

Chapter Thirty

"Something you might find quite interesting," Eva said, "Is the difference between Jewish and non-Jewish women and how they, and their communities, felt about women working." Eva was best friends with Yvonne's daughter. A few years ago, after a long search through her own family history, she started a company organising private, guided tours through Amsterdam. One of the most popular was the Diamond History tour and she'd been more than happy to tailor it to help Sarah with her search for Camille. "Dutch women in the 1940s," Eva continued, "in general, only worked out of necessity. Socially they were not expected to work, only if there wasn't any other option. However, for Jewish women it was quite normal and socially accepted, encouraged even, to work and therefore contribute to a better life for their families. A lot of Jewish women worked in retail, textile or, as Clara did, in the diamond industry."

Sarah looked at Yvonne, relieved she no longer had to do all of it on her own. The tour had been great so far and given her more information and places to search than she could have ever found herself.

"Diamond polishers didn't make a full-time wage from the job but it was enough for women to make their family's lives that little bit better."

"Do the factories still keep documentation of the people who used to work for them?" Sarah asked.

"There is a lot of documentation that survived and it's kept in two places, the Diamond Workers Union Archive and the City Archives." Eva said, "So there is a chance that you can find Clara in either of those."

After the diamond factory and a walk through the area of the city where, before the war, mostly Jews lived, Eva dropped them off at the city archive.

"I would start here. Archives can be tricky beasts to search but there is always someone here to help who knows where to look."

"Thanks, Eva. You've been a great help. I very much appreciate it."

"You're more than welcome and good luck. Let me know when you find her."

When you find her. Those words repeated in Sarah's head as she walked into the archives with Yvonne. She was confident and excited about getting closer and closer to finding out what happened.

The archivist started searching through the Diamond Workers Union's Archives and came up with a few Claras but most of them weren't of the right age. With every Clara they dismissed, Sarah's confidence started to crumble again. But then the last record was of a Clara who was born in the same year as her nanna and she worked as a diamond polisher.

"This could be her." Sarah said. She looked at Yvonne who had a twinkle in her eyes and they both leaned forward as the archivist made sure there weren't any others they hadn't yet looked at.

"So, who we have here is Clara Mol. She is the only one in the register of the right age and she worked as a diamond polisher, which matches the entry in the ledger you found." Sarah shuffled in her chair. They were getting close, they had a surname to look for now. But she also felt a sense of dread that if this wasn't the right Clara then this could well be the end of the search.

"What we don't have is any sign of Camille Mol. I've checked the city archives, as you did as well Sarah, but she isn't there." Yvonne put her hand on Sarah's arm and squeezed gently. "We know Camille was born during the war, so, at the time, she, most likely, wouldn't have been registered as it was far too dangerous. If she did survive, there are many possibilities why we can't find a record of her. It doesn't necessarily mean she didn't live to see the end of the war."

"It just means we won't be able to find her," Sarah said.

"I want to check one more record to see if we can find Clara and Camille there. It's a central database of holocaust victims and it's the most comprehensive record of victims from all over the world." Sarah waited as the archivist searched for Clara and when she turned her screen around for Sarah to see she knew the news wasn't good. The entry confirmed that Clara Mol was born in Amsterdam and that she was murdered in the holocaust.

184

She was transported to the Auschwitz extermination camp on 2 January 1945 and died on 25th March 1945.

After a long silence, Sarah cleared her throat. "So, if the dates in the diary are correct, and I have no reason to believe they're not, this is not the Clara we're looking for. It was February when Clara knocked on my nanna's door. And, by that time, this poor woman was already in Auschwitz."

"Is there an entry for a Camille in this database?" Yvonne asked.

After a few minutes of searching, the archivist put her hands down next to her keyboard.

"I found a few but none of the right age."

Sarah's shoulders slumped. Her only lead hadn't produced any information.

"Don't give up, Sarah," Yvonne said. "I know you were hoping to find more today but if Camille isn't in the database, there's a good chance she survived." The archivist nodded but Sarah shook her head.

"I know but that doesn't mean I'll find her. I think it might be time to give up."

Chapter Thirty-One

Amsterdam, February 1945

All the way home Louise repeated the address Frank made her memorise in her head. Nothing was written down, and if it was, it was burned as soon as possible.

"What if I get caught?" She asked Frank before making her way back through the supply cupboard. She was almost sure that he knew about Clara, he might even have arranged for her to knock on Louise's door. But her question of who'd look after her if Louise got caught hung unspoken in the air.

"Don't worry, Louise, just don't get caught."

When she got home, the urge to write the address down was hard to resist. She had to deliver the package between 10 and 10:30 the following morning. What if she woke up and couldn't remember? What if she got the numbers muddled up? She considered telling Clara but anyone other than her and Frank knowing would increase the risk. She'd have to trust her memory.

***

If she walked quickly, it'd take her about 20 minutes to get to the address she still remembered when she'd woken up this morning. Her memory wasn't the only thing she was grateful for this morning. The sun was shining and, even though it was cold, at least she didn't have snow or rain to contend with. She did her very best to avoid soldiers and to not make eye contact when she couldn't. She walked at a good pace but not so quick it looked like she was rushing.

When she knocked on the door she avoided looking around her. As it opened, she picked up Anna, grabbing the pillow at the same time. As Frank recommended, she greeted the man opening the door as if he were a close friend by giving him 3 kisses on his cheeks. He let her in and asked if she would like a glass of water.

"It's better if you don't go straight away. Less suspicious in case someone is watching."

Louise handed over the package and watched as the man put it in a tall cupboard. He seemed to open at least three doors before he put the package in. Louise wondered what else was hidden inside. She drunk her water and gratefully accepted a small piece of stale bread.

After half an hour of small talk about the weather, rations and how long they thought the war might go on for - neither knew enough to guess -, the man stood up, shook Louise's hand and thanked her for coming. The fear Louise had felt on the way there was gone. Even if she were stopped now, there was nothing to discover. Walking home, she struggled to figure out how she was feeling. Relieved, of course, but also a little deflated. She was so desperate to fight and all she did was go for a walk and have a chat and some bread and water.

"Well, I think you are really brave," Clara said when they came down later that afternoon. "Fighting doesn't always mean you need a gun. Everything you do for me, for Frank, it's all fighting. All the things you, and others, are doing will, eventually, end this war. Believe me, you are fighting."

A little spark of pride bounced around in Louise's chest. Maybe Clara was right.

Chapter Thirty-Two

"Do you want to do it or shall I?"

Paul hesitated. He still wasn't sure how he felt about clearing out Emma's room. Deep down he knew it was the right thing to do, the only way they could both get some closure and, maybe, move on. They'd been busy all day carefully packing up her clothes and toys. Now it was getting dark and the nightlight had come on for, what would be, the last time.

"Let's do it together." Sarah said as she took Paul's hand and nodded.

Paul swallowed hard, she looked so beautiful in the pink glow of the little light. He was glad she was on her way to be happy again, even if it was without him. She deserved it and if he was totally honest with himself, he'd been relieved, in a way, Sarah had been brave enough to end things. He knew he'd never have had the courage to be the one to do it, no matter how clear it'd become they had no future together.

"On the count of three?"

"One"

"Two"

"Three"

The click of the socket switch that, now, no longer powered the nightlight, sounded as loud as a crack of thunder in a quiet night.

"Have you found a new place yet?" Sarah asked. They were still sitting on the floor in Emma's room. Both unwilling to leave.

"I'm going to stay with my sister for a bit."

"In Edinburgh?"

"Yes," Paul told her that his boss had asked him to help them set up a new office in Scotland and run it for them. It seemed like a good opportunity, not only for his career but also a real chance of a fresh start. For both of them.

***

"How was it?" Jack asked as he twirled a strand of Sarah's hair between his fingers. Her head was resting on his legs and she turned onto her back to look at him.

"Awful. But good at the same time."

Jack bent down and kissed her forehead.

"I'm glad you're here," he said.

"Me too."

Sarah looked around Jack's living room. The huge dark brown corner sofa was soft and the crackling fire gave the gave the room a warm glow.

"I like your house," she said. "It's like a dressing gown."

Jack raised an eyebrow.

"You know," Sarah continued. "It makes you feel all wrapped up in cosiness." Jack laughed.

"I'll remember that one, for when I want to sell up."

"Why would you ever want to sell this place?"

"I don't know, maybe, one day on my travels, I'll meet the girl of my dreams. Maybe we'll fall in love at first sight."

"It sounds like you've got it all figured out."

"Well, maybe I've already met her," Jack leaned over and kissed Sarah.

"Do you think?" Sarah asked, trying to conceal her flushed cheeks.

"It wouldn't surprise me."

Sarah shut her eyes and snuggled closer, wondering how serious he was.

"What about you? What are your plans?" Jack asked.

Sarah sat up, crossed her legs on the sofa, took a cushion and cuddled it on her lap.

"Long term, I don't know. For now, I want to sort out my mum's stuff, and stay in the house for a bit longer. It feels good to be there."

"Do I feature in any of this?" Jack asked.

Sarah tried to catch his eyes but he was staring into the fire.

"It wouldn't surprise me," she said.

"Funny." Jack flashed her his cheeky grin and pulled her back onto his lap.

***

Paul sat on the floor in the middle of Emma's empty room. After Sarah left, he'd put all of Emma's clothes and toys in the boot of his car to take to the charity shop in the morning. Her cot and the rest of her furniture were in the hallway, dismantled, waiting to be picked

191

up. The only thing that remained in the room were memories of the long, sleepless nights, nappy changes and the cuddles.

On his phone, he scrolled through the photos the estate agent had taken the day before. How different things looked now.

Chapter Thirty-Three

Amsterdam, February 1945

"What are you making for dinner today?"

Adrenaline raced through Louise's body as she did her best to answer as calmly as possible.

"The usual, Frank."

In addition to going to the soup kitchen on Monday and Thursday, Frank had requested her to come as soon as possible on a day when he asked her this seemingly innocent question. Her response had been agreed as well to make it sound like a joke between friends. She knew the innocent exchange meant something far more important. She was needed, urgently.

"We need you to pick up something," Olaf said as soon as she'd made it through the pantry and into the cellar. Louise looked around for Frank but he wasn't there. She had to deal with the German soldier alone. She knew Frank wouldn't trust someone who didn't deserve it, still, she'd rather he'd been there.

"From where?"

Olaf gave her the address which was much further away than she normally had to go and gave her directions as she wasn't entirely sure where it was.

"After that, we need you to deliver it to an address in the city centre. It needs to be there before midday. Can you do that?"

It was tight but if she left straight away and walked fast, she could do it.

"You can count on me," she said as she bent down to pick up Anna's cuddly toy which had fallen to the floor. When she got up, Olaf had gone. There must be another way out of this cellar, she thought. She'd have noticed it if he'd gone out the way she was going now. She was on a tight schedule though, no time to look for hidden passages.

There was a dark mood hanging over the city that day. The atmosphere had an oppressive and threatening feel to it. It sat heavy in the pit of Louise's stomach in the same way as when, in the middle of the night, she heard the bomber planes approach.

After she picked up the parcel from a shifty man with an even more nervous looking wife -they didn't seem the kind of people you'd imagine working for the resistance- she had half an hour left to drop it off. She didn't know what would happen if she didn't get there in time and she had no intention to find out. She walked as fast as she could without looking suspicious.

"They always stop people who look like they're rushing," Frank had told her before her first job. "Not only because they might think you're up to something, also just to bully. They'll stop you to make you late, for no other reason than their own amusement."

As she turned the corner that took her into the street where she needed to deliver the parcel, she almost bumped into a couple of soldiers. She, instantly, lowered her gaze, muttered an apology and tried to walk around them, but they blocked her way. One of them grabbed hold of the pram and instinctively, she looked up to see who was threatening her baby. Her eyes widened when she recognised Olaf, who, just over an hour ago, had given her the assignment.

"Where are you going?" he barked at her.

"I'm going to see a friend." Louise lowered her eyes again.

"Who is this friend?" asked the other soldier who'd started looking in the tray under the pram. Louise tried not to look at the pillow under Anna's head. Was this a trap? Was he waiting here, at the address where she was meant to make her delivery, only to arrest her?

"He's called Anton and he lives a few streets from here." Louise hoped they wouldn't ask her for an actual address or, even worse, make her point out the house and risk the lives of whoever's house she was unfortunate enough to choose.

When the soldier lifted up Anna's blanket and started feeling around in the pram, Louise looked up at Olaf, praying this was all a coincidence and he could still save her. The look in his eyes did not fill her with hope. Just as the other soldier's hands moved close to the cushion, Olaf pushed him aside, grabbed Anna out of the pram and shoved her into Louise's arms.

"Just take her to the station!" he shouted. "She's clearly up to something."

"What about the pram?"

"Leave the stupid pram here, unless you want to strap it to the roof of your car?"

The soldier didn't argue and pushed Louise in the back of the car. "Are you coming?" he asked Olaf.

"I'll join you at the station later. Just lock her up and leave her until I get back."

Louise wasn't sure whether to be scared or relieved. At least the package hadn't been discovered but she still couldn't be sure whether Olaf could be trusted. For now all she could do was give him the benefit of the doubt because the alternative wasn't something she dared consider.

At the police station, Louise was put in a cell where she was left to worry about what to do when Anna needed a clean nappy and what would happen to Clara and Camille if they didn't let her go.

For what felt like hours, she was left alone. There were three other cells she could see. All occupied. In the one next to her was a man whom she thought must be about Peter's age, but it was hard to say for sure. His face was swollen with bruises and he had cut lips. He was lying on the wooden bed, so still that Louise feared he might be dead. His blond hair was matted with blood and his arm laid in an awkward angle. He must have felt her eyes on him because he turned to face her, groaning with pain, and opened one eye. The other was swollen shut.

"It's not as bad as it looks," he whispered. Louise doubted that was true.

Just as she was about to ask what had happened to him, three soldiers came in. Louise shrank into the corner as far as she could, now terrified what would happen if they'd come for her. They marched to the cell next to hers and dragged the man out. Two of them had to hold him up, he could no longer walk himself. She saw him stifle a scream when they grabbed his broken arm. She squeezed her eyes shut. The pain on the man's face, and his brave attempt to hide it, made Louise fear for Peter. Was he locked up in a cell like this somewhere? Being beaten for information he might or might not have?

Chapter Thirty-Four

"You busy this evening?"

"I guess I am now :-)" Sarah replied *"In or out?"*

As usual Alice replied almost instantly. Sarah often wondered whether she ever put her phone down or if she held it all day, ready to reply to anyone immediately.

"Cool. In? At yours?"

"Shall I cook?"

"Oh yes, please. I'll be there at 7."

"With wine of course," Alice added quickly. Not that she needed to. Alice always brought wine. She was a Project Manager for the City of Amsterdam and worked non-stop from when she stormed into the office at 8 in the morning until she went home at 6.30, constantly running around making sure everyone did their jobs and everything was done on time. She was brilliant at it. Sarah had no idea how she was still reasonably sane after doing it for almost 20 years when even just one day would probably push her over the edge.

"It's all about leaving work at work," Alice said when Sarah had questioned how she wasn't stressed. Sarah could always count on Alice's optimism.

Since her trip to the diamond factory, Sarah had struggled to find positives in her life. A broken marriage, no family, no job, Jack in England and, what was most unsettling, no idea what to do next. She hoped that talking things through with Alice, who understood her almost better than she did herself, would help clear things up. It usually did. She'd been so busy over the last couple of weeks that she hadn't even spoken to Alice, they had a lot to catch up on.

***

"Is that lasagne I can smell?" Alice asked as she hugged Sarah and walked through to the kitchen inhaling the wonderful smell coming from the oven.

"It sure is."

When they were both at university, they'd have lasagne at Sarah's every Friday before they went out to celebrate the start of the weekend. They had fond memories of those years when they spent pretty much all of their time together. That was until Sarah got the chance to finish her music degree in London. Alice had been devastated but it was such a good opportunity, it would have been foolish of Sarah not to grab it. Little did they know she'd meet Paul and move to Suffolk the day after she graduated.

"I miss lasagne Friday," Alice said with a pout.

"Me too."

They sat down at the table to eat and wash it all down with plenty of wine which tasted a lot better than the one they used to have at uni.

"What did Linda say about the house?" Sarah asked.

"She is so happy. We both are. Thanks again, it really means a lot."

"There is one problem though." Sarah laughed at the worried look on Alice's face. "You'll have to share with me for the foreseeable future."

"Well, that's not a problem. You had me worried there for a second. Are you not going back soon?"

"We're selling the house." Sarah said quietly whilst keeping her eyes firmly on her dinner.

"You're selling?"

"Yep."

"Are you.... are you splitting up?" Alice asked carefully.

"We are." Sarah looked up and realised that, surprisingly, saying it out loud didn't make her feel upset at all, instead she felt light and kind of floaty, as if she'd downed a glass of champagne.

"I'm sorry, Sarah," Alice looked as if she was bracing herself for impact. But the crash didn't come.

"Don't be. It's okay. I'm much happier without him and I'm pretty sure he feels better without me. I'm sad about the house, it's going to be very tough to let go of it but it's the only way we can both move forward." She poured them both another glass of wine. "To be honest, I'm kind of relieved that I don't have to go back to England. I think I want to stay here."

"Well, I'll drink to that." After a short silence a cheeky grin spread over Alice's face. "So does that mean I can finally call him a bastard?" Sarah laughed and nearly choked on her wine.

"You can call him anything you like," she said as she held up her glass to Alice.

"Seriously, though," Alice said, "If you're staying, we'd totally understand if you didn't want us to move in."

"No, no, you're fine. I really don't want to sleep in my mum's old bedroom anyway so you might as well. And it means I don't have to worry about decorating, we can just let Linda loose on it."

"She'd love that. She would probably do the whole house if you let her."

"I might just do that. She'll have some help though."

"What do you mean? Don't tell me you've taken up decorating?"

"Good God, no! No, Jack's coming over to help with the move and do some painting. He should be on his way as we speak." Alice smiled when she saw the twinkle in her friend's eyes. "He finished the job he had to go back for and he thought we might want some help."

"Finally! I've been dying to meet handsome Jack!"

"Please, don't call him that to his face, you make him sound like a pirate!" Alice pulled a pretend upset face and they both laughed.

When they finished their dinner, Alice started cleaning up but Sarah stopped her and marched her to the sofa.

"You've worked hard enough all day. Sit down and let me pour you another glass."

"Thanks, Sarah," Alice said as she slumped down, clearly exhausted from a long day at work. She picked up a white album from the coffee table and held it up in the air.

"Is this the guest book from your mum's funeral?"

"Yes, it was delivered today but I haven't had a chance to look at it yet, I've been too busy. Have a look if you like." Whilst she was cleaning up, Sarah told Alice about her trip to the diamond factory.

"Sounds like an interesting day."

"It was, Yvonne has been such a great help."

"But?"

"I think I've reached the end of the search. The only Clara we found was killed in Auschwitz. I honestly don't think they survived the war, and even it they did, there's very little chance I'll ever find them."

"I'm sorry, Sarah."

"It's ok. I need to move on. I'd convinced myself there was this big secret or mystery that I needed to find out about but there isn't. My mum probably just thought I'd like to read the diary, find out about the time when she was a baby. I love that I now know about Clara and Camille before the memory of them was lost forever. I think that was all she wanted."

"Maybe," Alice said looking deep in thought. "Don't give up yet though, I think you will find her in the end." She said flicking through the guestbook. When Sarah finished cleaning up, she put a newly opened bottle of wine on the coffee table and sat down opposite Alice.

"I think it's better to leave the past in the past. The search has been exhausting, the constant hoping and then finding out nothing, I don't think I can cope with any more of it."

"There are some lovely messages in here, Sarah." When Alice turned to the next page she stopped reading and looked up at Sarah in disbelief.

"I found Camille!"

Chapter Thirty-Five

Amsterdam, February 1945

A little after the man was collected from his cell, a soldier, who looked no older than 15, brought Louise a cup of water and a little broth. Walking up to her cell, he scrunched up his nose. Anna had just soiled the only spare nappy Louise had.

"Please, I need a clean nappy for my baby," she begged. The boy ignored her and left.

Louise drank half of the water and dripped some in Anna's mouth using her finger. When the door opened again her head snapped up. Two soldiers were dragging in another young man and locked him in the cell next to her. She tried not to think about what happened to the previous occupant. Then she noticed Olaf standing in the doorway and a flutter of hope rushed through her body.

"I thought you were getting her some clean nappies, it stinks in here!" he barked.

Louise slumped back into the corner, he clearly wasn't coming to let her out.

"We haven't been able to find any yet, sir."

"Then let the woman go. I can't stand this smell!"

"But sir," one of the soldiers said.

"But what? You want to disobey a direct order?"

"No, sir," he said and opened Louise's cell. She tried to catch Olaf's eye as they marched her out but he didn't look her way.

Pulling the front door shut behind her, Louise locked it immediately. She went through the motions of changing Anna's nappy. The poor girl's bottom was red and raw. Louise gently cleaned her and put her in her cot where she fell asleep straight away. She knocked on the ceiling for Clara and went down to see if there was any food. It was past dinner time and neither had had anything since breakfast. Louise lifted a corner of the curtain covering the back door and peeked out. The moon was already out and so bright it was almost lighter outside than in. She was surprised to see Anna's pram outside with a little parcel on the pillow.

"What's that?" asked Clara as she walked into the kitchen.

"I don't know. It was outside in the pram."

"Why was the pram outside?"

"Long story," Louise said as she opened the little parcel. For a moment, she feared it was another parcel for her to deliver. Her mouth watered when she saw the two slices of white bread. She cut one slice in half for her and Clara to share and wrapped the other back up for the next day. They sat down in the back room which was even colder than normal but they didn't notice. Their whole beings were engulfed in the taste of the white bread in their mouths. They resisted the urge to gobble it up, instead, with their eyes closed, they took the smallest of bites and savoured them until they melted away. It wasn't until they swallowed the last crumb, that Louise told Clara some of the things she lived through, careful to leave out any details that could put anyone in danger.

"Will they still want you to help?" Clara asked.

"I don't know."

"Do you still want to?"

"If they need me, I can't let them down," she said, not feeling the confidence she tried to layer her voice with. She didn't dare think what could have happened had Olaf not been there today.

Chapter Thirty-Six

"What do you mean you've found Camille?" Sarah snatched the album out of Alice's hands.

"I found her. She's in here. She must have been at the funeral, Sarah."

"Anna was a wonderful person who was very much loved by all who knew her. Both people from here and now and especially from the past. Love, Camille."

"We found Camille! We found her!" Alice took the guestbook off her before she spilled wine all over it.

"It's got a phone number with it, Sarah, look."

"I can't believe we actually found her." Sarah sat down but within seconds got back up again.

"You need to phone her." Alice said.

"What, now? I don't know what to say." Sarah said pacing up and down the room.

"Just thank her for the message in the guestbook and see what she says."

"But what if she doesn't want to talk to me?"

"She wouldn't have left her phone number if she didn't, would she?" There was no arguing with that but now she had found Camille, she felt nervous and even a bit reluctant to talk to her.

"What if the truth sucks? Once I know, I can't go back."

"True, but your mum would not have left that diary out for you if she thought you wouldn't want to find out. If she had even the slightest clue that the truth could make you unhappy, she'd have burnt it and you know that. She wanted you to find out."

Sarah knew she was right.

"So, man up and phone Camille!"

"Hello, is this Camille?" Sarah asked with a shaky voice.

"No, it's not."

Sarah held her breath and the voice, that sounded far too young to be Camille, said, "But I think I know who you are."

Chapter Thirty-Seven

Amsterdam, March 1945

"Come on, sweetheart, have a little milk," Clara said to Anna trying her hardest to make the girl drink a little. Anna had been poorly for a couple of days now and Louise couldn't get her to have any milk. She'd been slightly more willing when Clara tried to feed her with Camille by her side, but now even that wasn't working anymore.

"You should take her to a doctor, Louise, she's not well at all."

"I know, I'll go as soon as she's had little to drink. She hasn't had any for hours."

"I'll give it a try, you get ready to go."

"Thank you, Clara, I'll take her to Doctor den Boer, he's been my parent's doctor for as long as I can remember. Hopefully he'll have time to see her."

"I'm sure he will. Try not to worry, she'll be fine," Clara said but the look in her eyes didn't match her words.

Louise had been to see her mother that morning to ask if she wanted to come and stay with her for a few days. She thought it might cheer her up and it would also help her with Anna. But her mother wasn't well herself. The death of her husband had hit her hard and on top of that she had now caught a nasty cold. Louise begged her to come with her so she could look after her, although she wasn't at all sure how she'd cope with someone else to care for. But she wanted to stay at home where she felt close to her husband. Reluctantly, Louise left her with a cup of hot water and the promise to come again as soon as she could.

Having Clara around, even if it was only for a few minutes at a time, made Louise's life a little easier. She was struggling with the lack of sleep and she didn't know what she would have done without her help. Clara had spent most of the day before and today downstairs to help out with Anna and to try and feed her as often as she could, but at night it was too risky. They recently heard about so many raids that were done in the early hours of the morning when everyone was still asleep. So, at night, Louise was on her own. In between the whining and rumbling of the bomber planes and trying to comfort Anna, she slept very little and the nights seemed like endless lakes of time stretched out in front of her. Her arms hurt from holding Anna but it was the only thing that stopped her from crying.

When Anna had finally drunk a little, Louise wrapped her up as warm as she could and left for the doctor's house. Despite her aching arms, she carried Anna rather than putting her in the pram, to try and keep her warm. She shuffled along, carefully avoiding the frozen puddles. One nearly caught her out, she had to grab hold of a lamp post to keep her on her feet. After that she walked even slower.

When she got to the doctor's house it was in complete darkness and no answer came when she knocked. She knocked again not knowing what to do if he wasn't home. After another knock a woman poked her head through the window of the house next door.

"They're not there," she shouted. "They were arrested yesterday."

Panic rushed through Louise's body.

"Apparently, they were hiding some Jews in their basement," added the woman. There was not a hint of sympathy in her voice and Louise wondered how some people could be that cold. "Stupid, if you ask me," the woman continued. "Putting your family at risk like that for some dirty Jews? No, not me, thank you very much."

Before Louise could ask if she knew any other doctors in the area, the woman had disappeared back inside. She stood on the pavement gently rocking Anna. She didn't know any other doctors and she was too weak and cold to go all the way to the hospital. She kissed Anna, still burning up with fever, on her forehead and started walking back home. She'd ask Mrs van Dijk if she knew someone who could help but when she knocked there was no answer there either. It was getting late and Louise could barely feel her fingers and toes.

She stared at Anna wrapped up in her arms. She would be okay for another day.

Chapter Thirty-Eight

"I'm Sophia. Clara's granddaughter."

"Clara's granddaughter?" Sarah fell silent, letting her brain process the information. "Does that make you…"

"That makes me Camille's niece."

Sarah didn't know what to say. Camille's niece. That meant that Clara survived to have another child after the war.

"My mother was Camille's younger sister."

"Did Camille survive the war?"

"She did."

Sarah felt the tingle of nerves in her fingertips.

"Is she still alive? Do you know where I can find her?"

Sophia didn't answer all her questions. Instead she invited Sarah to come over on Saturday with a promise to tell here everything she wanted to know.

***

The streets of Edinburgh welcomed Paul with an unfamiliarity that was like a healing balm spreading over his body and his soul. None of the people he'd met so far knew about Emma. Nobody gave him the 'tilted head look of sympathy' when he was anywhere near a baby. They also didn't know he'd failed to make his marriage work.

The landlord of the pub around the corner from his rented apartment was friendly and Paul enjoyed his company.

"Hey, Suffolk boy, here for dinner?"

"Yep," Paul replied as he sat down at the bar.

"You don't have a wife at home cooking for you?"

"Nope."

"Shame. Won't be long though, before the ladies round here will find out and start making work of you." Paul smiled and ordered a beer.

Life wasn't good quite yet, but it was certainly going in the right direction.

***

After Alice left, she called Jack to ask if he'd arrived yet.

"I just got through customs and was going to..."

"I found Camille!" Sarah interrupted him.

"You found her? How?"

Sarah told him what had just happened and that she arranged to go see Sophia the next day.

"Will you come with me?"

"I'd love to but what time do we have to leave? Not too early, I hope. It's just that it's quite a way from the hotel to yours and I forgot to bring my alarm clock with me."

Sarah realised where he was going with this and she smiled.

"Oh dear, that is a problem. I can always call you in the morning to make sure you're awake?"

"That won't work as I always switch my phone off at night." She could almost hear the cheeky grin she loved so much drip from his voice.

"I'm not sure what to suggest then. Unless you want to come and stay here tonight? I have a spare room and I could make sure you are up in time."

"I think that would be best. But maybe I should sleep in your room, it's going to be chilly tonight and I wouldn't want you getting cold." Sarah laughed out loud.

"You're quite something, Jack Rogers. Better make your way over here before it gets too cold for you to go out."

"Won't be long!" Before Sarah could say bye he'd hung up. She shook her head and smiled as she put her phone away.

Chapter Thirty-Nine

Amsterdam, March 1945

At the first sign of light, Louise had wrapped Anna in her blanket and went out to see Mrs van Dijk who made her a hot drink and gave her directions to her nephew's house. Proudly, she'd told Louise how he'd qualified as a doctor just before the start of the war and how he, despite his lack of experience, was trying to help as many people as he could. Louise was grateful to at least have somewhere to go for help. It would be a long walk but she had no other choice. Anna was getting worse and had stopped feeding completely. She had to go.

The small cup of broth she'd had for breakfast this morning, which was all the food she had left, was nowhere near enough to give her the energy to walk that far. Every few minutes she had to stop and lean on a lamppost to steady herself. The light-headedness caused by the lack of both food and sleep slowed her down and it took nearly an hour and a half to finally get to the doctor's house. Please let him be home, she muttered when she knocked on the door. The door was quickly opened by the doctor himself. He looked at Anna's little face and ushered them in before Louise could even explain who'd sent them. In the living room, he gently took Anna from Louise's arms and laid her down on a table to examine her. As he listened to her lungs his face showed a worried frown.

"It looks like a chest infection or even pneumonia." The doctor passed Anna back to Louise to put her dress back on.

"But don't worry, Louise, I've just managed to get my hands on a supply of penicillin so we should be able to get Anna back to feeling a little better soon."

"Thank you, doctor," she said as she felt the tension flow from her shoulders. Anna would be fine. She'd get better.

"If she doesn't show improvement in the next 12 hours you need to take her straight to hospital, Louise. She's really poorly but you did the right thing by bringing her here. Keep her as warm as you can and feed her often, she's lost a lot of fluids."

"Thank you," Louise said again.

"You're welcome. I hope Anna feels better soon."

Getting back home was almost too much for Louise. When she finally got back, she tripped on the steps leading up to the house and nearly fell inside when she opened the door. The house felt warm compared to the freezing temperature outside although she could still see her breath coming out of her mouth in cold clouds. She gave Anna her medicine and took her upstairs. After sitting in the chair next to the cot for half an hour, rocking Anna gently in her arms, she seemed a lot calmer and it looked like she was finally in a deep sleep rather than the restless naps she'd been having since she had gotten ill. Maybe the medicine had started working already. She was worried that Anna hadn't had any milk since they'd gotten back from the doctor and she couldn't quite remember when she last fed. She should try and feed her but she looked so very peaceful, waking her up didn't seem like the right thing to do. She'd try as soon as she stirred. That was Louise's last thought as she got into bed and fell fast asleep. It was a deep dreamless sleep. After days of just dozing for a few minutes here and there in between trying to feed a screaming Anna, the quietness of the room allowed Louise to finally rest undisturbed.

Chapter Forty

"What will I say to her?" Sarah asked as they walked up to the garden path.

"Just tell her what happened. Tell her about the diary and ask her whether she knows why your nanna stopped writing. She must know something worth telling you otherwise why would she try to get in touch?"

"True. Thank you for coming with me. I think I would have chickened out by now if you weren't here." Jack kissed her on the top of her head.

"Don't worry, I won't let you give up now." Do you want me to come in with you or shall I wait out here?" Sarah felt bad for leaving him to wait outside for her, especially after asking him to come along, but she needed to do this on her own.

"I'll be here if you need me. I won't go far."

Sarah took a deep breath. "Wish me luck," she said as she walked down the path of the lovingly maintained front garden. There were clumps of crocuses trying their best to brighten things up until the daffodils and tulips would take over. When she got to the front door, she stood there for a few seconds as she gathered the courage to knock. She looked back at Jack who gave her a thumbs up. When she finally did knock, the door was opened almost immediately.

The woman standing in the doorway was about her age, maybe a few years younger, and Sarah was surprised to see she reminded her a little of herself. The two of them stood and looked at each other in silence for a moment as if they were deciding whether they already knew each other or not.

"Hi, Sarah, I'm Sophia. Please, come in."

"Thank you so much for seeing me," Sarah said. She followed Sophia through the hallway into a bright but cosy living room.

"Would you like a coffee?"

"That would be lovely, thank you."

"Make yourself at home, I'll be just a minute."

Sarah sat down on a light grey sofa that looked soft and comfortable without being imposing. The white walls made the room feel bigger than it was and the pale green window frames and light oak furniture gave it a Nordic feel. It looked effortlessly stylish. The sideboard on the opposite end of the room was crowded with framed photos. Sarah was curious and got up to have a peek. She picked up a photo in a plain wooden frame and stared at it until her eyes hurt. She was glued to the image and didn't notice Sophia coming back into the room with a tray filled with cups, a pot of coffee and some biscuits. Sophia put the tray on the table and gently touched her on the arm.

"Are you okay?"

Sarah snapped out of her frozen state. "Why do you have a photo of my mum?" She was so shocked that she couldn't make her blunt question sound a little more friendly.

"That's not your mum, Sarah, that's mine. That's my mum." Sarah looked at Sophia for a long time, unsure of what to say or even think.

"I don't understand," was all she finally managed. Sarah sat back down on the sofa unable to peel her eyes off the image she thought had been her mum.

"I don't understand," she said again, quieter now. The woman in the photo looked almost identical to her mum although now she'd been told it wasn't, she could see small differences. Sarah wasn't sure why tears were welling up in her eyes but she was incapable of holding them back. Sophia handed her a tissue.

"Are you ready to hear Camille's story?"

Chapter Forty-One

Amsterdam, March 1945

Louise woke up to the noise of a plane rumbling overhead. She clenched her hands together and mumbled a prayer for it not to drop any bombs. When the sound had reduced to a distant murmur, she exhaled and noticed the silence. The room was pitch black; she must have slept for hours. Memories of her long walk to take Anna to see the doctor were slowly seeping into her consciousness. Why was she so quiet? Was it the medicine? Was it working already and making her sleep so soundly? Louise couldn't remember the last time she woke up without the sound of crying. Suddenly wide awake and worried she rushed over to Anna's cot.

Even in the darkness she could tell something was very wrong. She was so still. Louise reached to touch her forehead, the way she'd done hundreds of times since

Anna had fallen ill. She pulled her hand back as soon as her fingers made the slightest contact with her skin. Her little forehead felt like ice. Louise picked her up and cuddled her tight, but Anna's tiny limp body didn't react to anything. Another bomber plane flew over the city, this one came very low down and its deafening roar coincided with Louise's scream. A raw animal howl that easily overpowered the noise of the plane. Clara came rushing down the ladder and sped into Louise's bedroom where she put her arms around her and gently rocked her until she stopped screaming. Clara took Anna out of her arms and laid her in her cot. Louise stood motionless next to the little bed, staring but not seeing anything. Clara led her out of the room and downstairs where she made a little fire with the very last book that was left. Louise sat quietly whimpering with her head in her hands. Clara gave her a glass of water and went back to Louise's bedroom. She wrapped Anna in her blanket, leaving only her face visible, brought her up into the attic, for once grateful for the cold, and laid her down on her own bed for now. She picked up Camille to go back downstairs and gave Anna a kiss on her cold forehead.

"Sleep tight, my lovely girl."

In the doorway to the back room she hovered, unsure of what to do. Louise needed her and she couldn't leave Camille all the way up in the attic on her own but she didn't want to cause Louise even more hurt. Quietly she moved the basket Anna and Camille had shared so often out of Louise's line of sight and put Camille down. She sat down opposite Louise and took her hand. Only then did Louise look up. Camille stirred in the basket and Clara stiffened.

"I'm sorry, I couldn't leave her in the attic."

Louise smiled without it reaching her eyes.

"She should be in front of the fire. She'll get cold."

Clara moved the basket but kept it out of Louise's sight as much as possible.

All night they sat in silence, with the only thing breaking it being Louise's grief. It came in waves of first stillness and then endless tears. When Louise cried Clara held her tight until she could control the need to scream out her pain. And then the quiet numbness returned again.

"I'll leave tonight," Clara said after hours of silence.

Louise looked up in shock. Her eyes red and raw. "Don't go. You can't leave me alone now."

"We can't stay, Louise, you need to give Anna a proper burial and we can't stay here after that. People will hear Camille cry, it's too dangerous."

"Please stay, please!" Louise's shoulders started shaking. She couldn't bear the thought of being all alone in this big house. In the short amount of time she'd known them, Clara and Camille had become the most important people in her life, she had to keep them safe. She'd never forgive herself if something happened to them. Camille had to survive otherwise all would have been for nothing. Louise had lost far too many people already. She had to protect her.

"Please, stay," she said again. "Promise you'll stay?"

"We'll stay, if you're sure."

"I'm sure, I can't do this without you."

"We'll work something out. Together. I promise." Clara hugged Louise who clung to her so tight she could barely breathe.

When the night was losing ground to the morning, Louise wiped her eyes and sat up straight. "We'll bury her in the garden."

"Oh, Louise," was all Clara said.

"I have to keep her close. I don't want her in a graveyard far away. She has to stay here with me."

***

"I think it's deep enough," Louise said.

They'd been digging for hours. So far the moon had been behind dark clouds hiding everything. It was so dark that they'd had to feel their way to the edge of the patio. Shuffling forward feeling with their feet for the soil to start.

"Let's go a little deeper," Clara said

It was slow progress. Neither had the strength for digging and the ground was still frozen in places. Just after 2 o'clock in the morning they both put down their spades.

"Are you sure you want to do this?" Clara whispered.

Louise's throat felt too tight to answer. She picked Anna up and kneeled down besides the tiny grave. She squeezed her tight and then gently placed her in the hole.

"Sleep tight, poppet," was all she could manage.

Thud.

Clara had picked up her spade again and started filling up the hole.

Thud.

Louise leaned forward until her forehead nearly touched the ground, her tears slowly saturating the soil.

Thud.

Thud.

She didn't look up until Clara kneeled next to her and patted the soil.

"It's done," Clara said as she marked the grave with two pebbles. She gently raised Louise up and guided her back inside.

"I will keep you safe, Clara," Louise said as Clara put her to bed. "You and Camille. You will be safe."

Clara tucked her in. "I know," she said but Louise was already asleep.

Chapter Forty-Two

"So you're saying that my nanna's baby, Anna, died during the war?" Sarah asked, unsure of how to process this information. How could her mum have died as a baby?

"Yes, Anna was only 4 months old when she died. It was a tragedy, one which, I'm sure, very much influenced both Louise's and Clara's decisions that followed." Sophia looked at Sarah to check if she was okay to continue.

"They buried her in the back garden, both to keep Anna close to Louise, who was unwilling to let go of her, and to make sure nobody would find out about Clara and Camille. They hid Anna's death from everyone. Even Louise's mum who was, at that point, so ill Louise didn't want to break her heart even more."

"That must have been so hard, to not only lose your child but to then not be able to tell anyone, not even your mum." Sarah started to understand why her nanna didn't want to talk about this dreadful time in her life.

She couldn't imagine keeping such a horrific secret. When Emma died, the one thing that got Sarah to finally move on was being able to talk about it. Her mum, Alice, friends in England, they all spent hours and hours listening to her and encouraging her to keep going. To go outside, to laugh, to cry and all the while telling her she was brave enough to get through another day. If you didn't have that, how could you cope with such a tragedy in any way other than to lock it away so deep inside, hoping that maybe, one day, you'd forget yourself? She felt sorry for being so angry at her nanna for not talking. How could she have talked? How could she, after all that time, let it out and live through it all over again? Sarah, better than anyone, now understood.

"It was extremely difficult for Louise. My nan, Clara, told me she insisted on leaving so Anna could have a proper funeral but Louise didn't want to hear a word about it. She begged her to stay and became almost obsessed with keeping Camille safe."

"Do you know where in the garden they buried her?"

"I do. The morning after Louise had woken up to find Anna had died in her sleep, she was sitting at the table in the back room with Clara trying to figure out what to do. It was an impossible situation for both of them but they had no choice other than to deal with it. When Louise opened the curtains and said she would bury Anna in the garden they both looked out and saw the sun peeping over the fence leaving a little spot of sunlight in the middle of the garden. My nan told me it was as if the sun was pointing out a spot to them." Sarah shivered and told Sophia about Emma and the olive tree she planted for her and how she felt whilst digging in the ground.

228

Sarah wished her mum would have told her what her nanna went through. Not only would it have probably improved the relationship she had with her, it might also have helped her deal with the loss of Emma. She looked at Sophia, there was a question she needed to ask but she wasn't sure how to. She was scared to find out the truth. Sophia waited patiently until she gathered enough courage to ask.

"I don't understand how Anna could have died though. My mum was born in November 1944, after my grandad had to go on the run. He never got to see his daughter. Or at least that's what I was always told." She held on to the side of the sofa as if that could stop her whole world, as she knew it, from tumbling down around her.

"You have to understand that the situation our grandmothers found themselves in is one we cannot easily understand. It was an extremely brutal time and neither of them had their husbands, or anyone else for that matter, to turn to for help or advice. Both of them were trying to do the best they could to not only survive, but to also do the right thing. And at that time with all the misery, the hunger, the cold and the utter cruelty of the Nazis, knowing what was right wasn't always easy. Louise had recently lost her father in such a horrific way that it was impossible to imagine how she felt and her mum was so ill she feared for her life too. On top of all that she'd just lived through the heartbreaking tragedy of losing her baby. And for Clara nothing was certain other than that she had to protect Camille and she owed both their lives to Louise."

Sarah tried to imagine how she'd cope in those circumstances but she couldn't. Her nanna would've been a few years younger than she was now when all this happened. So young and still unequipped to deal with everything that was thrown at her.

"Do you want to hear the rest?" Sophia asked.

"I do, of course I do. It's just all a bit overwhelming."

"Just take a minute and let me know when you're ready to hear it. Take your time. There is no rush."

"I have brought a friend," Sarah said realising how silly it sounded but she wasn't sure she was ready to hear the rest on her own. "He's waiting outside."

"Why don't you go and get him? It might help you to be with someone you know when you hear the end of the story."

Sarah went outside to find Jack. As promised, she didn't have to look far. He was sitting on a bench on the other side of the road under a large tree which looked at least a hundred years old. She looked at its impressive trunk and far reaching branches and wondered about the things it must have seen in its time, how much pain it had witnessed. She waved Jack over and when he reached her, she grabbed his hand.

"I need you," was all she said. Jack squeezed her hand and walked into the house with her. Sarah introduced him to Sophia and when Sophia went to make him a drink he whispered into Sarah's ear, "Have you seen her eyes, they're just like yours."

"I know," Sarah whispered back. When Sophia came back with Jack's coffee she filled him in on everything she had told Sarah so far.

"I don't get it, didn't you say your nanna only had one child?" he asked.

"We were just getting to that bit," Sophia said.

"I guess what you're going to tell me next will explain that photo as well?" Sophia nodded.

Sarah showed Jack the photo of Sophia and her mum and one of her own mum she carried in her purse. He looked confused. "They could be twins."

"Your nanna was a very brave woman who single-handedly saved the life of both my nanna and her little girl Camille. When Clara knocked on her back door with a baby on a freezing winter's night in 1945, Louise let them in and gave them a place to hide. She fed them, kept them as warm as she could, made clothes for baby Camille, shared whatever she had with them and all the while making Clara feel part of her family. It wasn't just a hiding place she offered them, she gave Clara back her faith in the kindness of people. Even in the harshest circumstances imaginable, when everyone Louise held dear was taken from her, she still did everything she could to keep them safe, right up to the moment Clara escaped arrest and certain death, again thanks to your nanna."

Sarah told Sophia about her meeting with Marijke and she showed her Frank's ledger. Sophia looked through it and stopped on the page that held her grandmother's name.

"My nan told me about Frank and how she always felt guilty for not getting in touch after the war to thank him for all he did for her."

"How did they escape?" Jack asked.

"At the end of March 1945 there was a door-to-door raid in the early hours of the morning. Louise was awake and saw them coming. This gave Clara just

231

enough time to escape through the attic window and down the drain pipe. She climbed over several fences before she hid under a bush until the night went quiet and she continued her escape. Eventually she hid in a coal shed and fell asleep."

"She did all that with a baby?" Sarah asked.

"No," said Sophia. "She wouldn't have made it if she'd taken Camille."

Chapter Forty-Three

Amsterdam, March 1945

Louise hadn't slept properly since Anna died. She couldn't bear to be in the room where it happened. Where she'd lost everything. She'd opened up the living room again so she could, at least, rest on the sofa at night. It was still cold but spring was on its way and would hopefully soon bring warmer weather. She tried everything to keep the memories of that awful night at bay but nothing worked. As soon as she fell asleep the nightmares started. She dreamed about rushing to hospital with Anna, carrying her blue, limp body through the snow, never getting there in time. Other nights, her guilt for falling asleep while her baby was dying, maybe, if she'd been awake, she could have saved her, played up as soon as she shut her eyes. She'd dream of Anna as a toddler, an age the poor girl would never see, lying dead on the floor. Louise would rush to her and just before she'd scoop her up in her arms, Anna would open her eyes and say: "It wasn't your fault, mama." The dreams were far worse than the tiredness, so she stayed awake.

During the day, Louise pretended to the rest of the world that everything was fine. When she went out to get her rations, she brought a very well wrapped up Camille with her, constantly worrying that someone would see that this wasn't Anna. But nobody did. Nobody noticed this wasn't her darling girl, nor could they tell that every little noise from Camille cut through her like a ragged piece of glass that was so painful you'd wish for the clean cut of a sharp knife. Nobody noticed her daughter was gone forever. Pretending Clara's little girl was her own was one of the hardest things Louise had ever done. Cuddling her to keep her warm and giving her back when she got home felt like ripping out her heart. But she had no choice, this was the only way she could keep Camille safe.

At night the grief for Anna strangled her. Every night, after she fed Camille, who was now sleeping in Anna's cot, Clara sat with Louise for a while. She had been worried about it being too painful to have Camille sleeping where Anna should have been but Louise insisted. She didn't want the little girl sleeping in the cold attic when there was an empty cot right there. Keeping Camille safe was the only thing that kept her going. It gave her a purpose, a reason to get up and do all the things she no longer cared about but she had to keep doing to survive. It was also safer. If there was a raid, a cry from the attic would mean the end for all three of them, whilst a baby in Anna's cot was expected as nobody knew she was no longer there.

Louise was sitting on the sofa holding her head. It hurt so much it felt like someone was pounding her with a block of concrete. Clara was quietly talking to Louise about anything she could think of to try and distract her from the pain. Together they sat on the sofa under Louise's blanket sharing the stillness of the night. After a while Louise noticed Clara was no longer talking. She had fallen asleep. Louise covered her with the blanket and walked to the kitchen for a glass of water. Peeking through the curtain covering the back door she stared out into the garden. The full moon was so bright Louise could see everything as clear as if it was daylight. Had it been four nights since they had been out there digging? Or five? She couldn't remember. It was hard to keep track of the days and the nights were so long her sense of time could no longer be trusted. She looked at the spot again and tried to push away the image of Anna's little body wrapped in her blanket deep in the cold ground. But it wouldn't go. It was there whenever she blinked. The image and the sound of the dirty soil falling on her sweet baby girl would haunt her forever.

In the living room, Louise looked at Clara with envy. What she wouldn't give to be able to sleep so peacefully? But their night was far from over.

A noise outside woke Louise with a start. She must have nodded off for a while. Clara was still asleep. There was banging, crying, shouting. She made a small gap in the curtains and looked out. The scene she saw outside made fear rush through her body and her legs turn to jelly. There were soldiers everywhere. Banging on doors, bursting into houses as soon as their doors opened even a tiny bit, or breaking them down if they weren't opened quick enough. She saw people being dragged out of their houses and rounded up under the big chestnut tree, the only tree that had survived in her street because it was just too big to chop down. Guns pointed at them. A truck waiting to take them away.

"Clara!" she hissed. "Clara, wake up! You have to go!"

Clara jumped up off the sofa. Blood had drained out of her face and she looked like a ghost standing in the dark room. She seemed unable to move.

"There's soldiers everywhere, Clara! Get Camille and hide in the garden! Quick!" Clara snapped out of her shocked state and started moving. She hugged Louise hard. "I owe you forever," she whispered in her ear and started running up the stairs. Louise heard her rush up the stepladder and pull it up before she closed the hatch.

How could she have gotten Camille so quickly? And why was she going up in the attic? She needed to come down and hide in the garden. They'd find her upstairs. Louise had no time to think. The soldiers were outside her house. Even though she knew it was coming she gave a yelp when they hammered on her door. She ran to open it as quick as her jelly legs allowed.

"Aufmachen!" The soldiers shouted as they assaulted the door again. When she opened it, three of them marched in and pushed her back into the living room. "Sit!" One shouted as he pushed her towards the sofa. Louise tripped on the corner of the rug and fell down on her knees. She scrambled back up and stumbled to the sofa. A soldier stood over her with a gun pointing at her head whilst the other two searched the house. Louise clasped her shaking hands together, kept her face down and focused on her beloved rug. She'd spent ages getting the previous boot prints out. Maybe she'd just throw it out and get a new one as soon as this dreadful war was over, should she live to see that. Any second now they'd find Clara and it would all be over. Would they kill her on the spot or would she join the group under the tree? And what about her? Louise needed to keep her mind busy and not give in to the fear. To distract herself she started a mental list of chores she'd have to do in the morning, ignoring the fact she'd probably be dead by then.

As her list grew, the soldiers moved upstairs. A baby cried. When Louise heard them open the hatch she could no longer breathe. Her head spun and her vision blurred. She held onto the sofa as if bracing for impact. Shouting was coming from upstairs. She didn't recognise any of the words. Her body started shaking and tears were streaming down her cheeks. Soon, they'd bring Clara down, they'd all be dragged out of the house and rounded up under the tree with the others. Any moment now would be their last. The soldiers came running down the stairs. The front door slammed shut.

And then it was quiet.
Louise looked up.
The soldiers were gone.

Louise didn't move until the noise outside had died down and everything was quiet. She could hear no more shouting or banging. No more screaming and begging to be let go. Carefully, she looked out and saw empty streets. Whether they'd searched all the houses in her street or they'd found what they were looking for, she didn't know. There was nobody outside but she knew everyone would be awake. She looked down the road and noticed a couple of front doors had been left open but it didn't look like anyone was still inside. The soldiers must have not have shut them after arresting everyone inside. She would go out later, when she was sure it was safe, to close them. It wasn't right to just leave them open like that.

Louise realised she could still hear a baby cry. When she'd heard it earlier, she'd assumed it was coming from outside but the streets were empty now. It sounded like it was coming from upstairs. She walked up and into her bedroom. The crying was coming from Anna's cot. Camille was still there. Louise stood and looked at her, unable to figure out why she wasn't gone. She picked her up and the crying stopped.

"What are you still doing here, poppet?" Camille smiled and Louise kissed her on her forehead. "Don't worry little one, your mummy will come back for you as soon as it is safe." Louise stroked her little cheek and Camille grabbed hold of her finger. "And until then, you have me. I'll look after you." As if Camille knew that she was safe, she fell asleep and Louise put her back in the cot.

She sat down on the bed and watched her sleep, waiting for her brain to catch up with everything that happened in the last 10 minutes. Eventually, she gathered the courage to go up into the attic. She took the chair, opened the hatch and climbed up the ladder. The big empty space showed no sign of anyone having lived up here, nothing. The piece of fabric was no longer covering the little window which looked like it wasn't quite shut properly. She opened it and looked out. In the corner of the garden, on the ground, was a dark bundle. It hadn't been there before, a cushion and a blanket maybe? And was that the bucket that Clara had used as a toilet? She couldn't tell for sure, a cloud had moved in front of the moon and the night turned very dark indeed. She couldn't understand how Clara had managed to escape so quickly without leaving a trace but she was sure she'd come back.

Chapter Forty-Four

"She was on her own?" Jack asked and Sophia nodded.

"Clara knew she couldn't escape via the roof with Camille and she didn't have enough time to go downstairs and get out through the back door. The roof was the only way out. So, she made the second hardest and bravest decision of her life and she escaped without Camille. She left her baby girl safe in Anna's cot, under Louise's protection. It was her only option. If she had stayed, all three of them would have most likely been killed, or arrested at best. If she'd taken Camille with her, they wouldn't have made it. Until the day Clara died, she believed that it was the best decision for all of them."

"What happened to Clara?"

"When she woke up in the shed she had hidden in during her escape, she didn't know what to do. She waited for a while but she knew that, eventually, she'd have to come out. I remember her telling me that opening that shed door was one of the most terrifying moments of her life. There was no window, so she literally had no idea what she would find outside and she no longer had the cover of night to keep her safe. She took a deep breath, gathered all the courage she could muster and opened the door. There was nobody in the garden but soon as she stuck her head out and looked towards the house, she locked eyes with a woman in the kitchen. The woman didn't come out into the garden but, urgently, waved her over and unlocked the kitchen door to let her in. She was given a blanket, a cup of hot water and a place to sleep in the attic. No questions were asked. There was no need. Clara stayed with them until the end of the war. She found out later the people next door were known traitors who would have, no doubt, handed her over to the Nazis if it had been their shed she'd been hiding in. She was very lucky to survive."

Sarah and Jack were hanging on Sophia's every word.

"Clara's husband, Daniel, also survived and they found each other through the local synagogue shortly after liberation. They eventually managed to get their lives back on track and they lived happily into their eighties. Initially they both struggled to come to terms with everything that had happened to them, the war had had an enormous impact on their lives but they spent their days grateful for the people who helped them and they did what they could to repay what they owed; their lives."

Jack looked at Sarah to make sure she was okay. She took his hand and he knew then that she was strong enough to deal with whatever came next.

"You said that leaving Camille with Louise was the second hardest decision of Clara's life. What was the hardest?" Sarah asked. She felt the tension in the room heighten as they waited for the most important part of the story. She squeezed Jack's hand hard and he moved closer to her.

"I know this will be hard for you to hear at first, but knowing the truth will hopefully give you some peace." Sophia said. Sarah felt like this was one of these moments that would change your life forever.

"When the war ended, it was chaos for Clara. She had no money, no idea whether her husband or her family were still alive, and she had nowhere to live as the house they'd rented before the war was no longer theirs. She decided to leave Camille with Louise until they had a safe place for her. Clara hoped desperately that Louise didn't mind and she suffered a great deal of guilt in those early days as she could only imagine how hard it must have been for Louise looking after someone else's baby when she no longer had her own. When she found Daniel, they felt blessed to be so lucky to have both survived. But Clara struggled with the burden of owing Louise hers and Camille's life. She wanted nothing more than to pay the enormous debt she felt she owed her."

Chapter Forty-Five

Amsterdam, July 1945

It was a bright summer morning. It was already warm and the temperature was likely to rise to blistering heat within the next few hours. Louise walked with Camille happily sitting in the pram. Two months it had been since Amsterdam had become a free city once again and going outside without the risk of running into soldiers was still a bit of a novelty. Many found it hard to trust they were all gone.

***

It was only two days after liberation and it seemed the whole city had come to the main square to celebrate. The Dam was full of children dancing, which had been forbidden for the last three years of the war, to the sound of the street organs that were finally allowed to play again. Total strangers were hugging each other and the air was full of laughter. Louise hadn't heard so much joy in what felt like forever.

But then her ears filled with a noise that changed the atmosphere instantly. The short bursts of machine gun fire shocked everyone back into the fear they'd been so used to. Laughing was replaced by screaming. More gunshots. A short distance from Louise a man fell down, there was blood everywhere, some splattered to the side of Camille's pram. Without hesitation Louise ran. So did everyone else. In the panic to get away, many got trampled on, others tripped over prams and bicycles and were unable to get back up. Louise was lucky she'd been content watching the party from the edge of the square rather than join in herself, it meant she, now, had space to run.

She didn't stop until her lungs felt like they were exploding and she found herself in a quiet side street. Leaning forward with her hands on her knees she tried to catch her breath.

It wasn't until the next day she found out this wasn't the only shooting in the city. There were several other reports of German soldiers, whose weapons had not yet been confiscated, opening fire at unsuspecting citizens. Where there should have been celebrating, there was, again, only fear.

***

Louise stopped to pick up a toy that Camille had thrown out of the pram. It was the knitted bunny; Anna's favourite. She gave it back to her with a smile although her heart felt like it was being torn apart.

244

Clara could see them both clearly from the other side of the street where she was sitting on a bench pretending to read a newspaper. She was breathing calmly to make the queasiness she'd been feeling most mornings fade. When Louise didn't answer her knock on the door earlier, she'd decided to wait, it was such a beautiful day and Clara was more than happy to sit in the sun for a while. She could've approached Louise when she saw them come out of the bakery but she wanted to watch them for a while first.

When Camille appeared to look straight at her, Clara's breath caught and she risked a little wave. Camille smiled and Louise, not knowing what or who she smiled at, bent over to stroke her cheek. As Louise walked on, Clara crossed the road to follow them more closely. She felt bad for spying on them like this but it was so nice to see her baby girl so happy, she was reluctant to break the moment.

Again, Camille looked straight at her and Clara wondered whether her daughter would remember her.

"Mama," Camille said in a crystal-clear baby voice. Clara, who was only a few metres behind them, swallowed the lump that was tightening her throat. She was about to call out to them but Louise's answer stopped her.

"Clever girl saying mama. I'm not your mama though, sweetheart. I wish I was because I love you very much. Your mamma was very brave but I think the bad people caught her when she tried to escape. I don't think she made it. Don't worry though, my sweet. I will be your mama. You will never want for anything."

Clara stood still and watched them walk away. She never considered that Louise might have thought she was dead but it made perfect sense for her to assume the worst. After all, she hadn't been in touch since she'd climbed out of the attic window.

***

When she found Daniel, shortly after the war had ended, they had nothing but they managed to get themselves back on track. If there was anything the occupied years had taught them, it was how to survive against all odds. They found a little flat to rent and Daniel had been given a job by the council sweeping streets and collecting rubbish. Money was tight but they had enough to get by. They paid their rent, got their food rations and even managed to buy some second hand clothes. The feeling of clean clothes against her skin was heavenly and it made Clara feel like life was almost back to normal again. They tried to put some money aside as they would need it pretty soon. Clara was late with her monthlies. Life was almost perfect. There was only one thing missing: Camille. They had a safe place for her now. She could come home. Leave Louise and Peter to get on with their own lives without having to look after someone else's baby.

***

Clara couldn't take her eyes off Camille. She looked so happy. Louise was stopped by someone and they started chatting. Clara thought she'd approach her after they'd finish talking. It'd be rude to interrupt.

"I was so sorry to hear about Peter, Louise. He was far too young to be taken away from you both. How are you coping on your own?"

Peter was dead? Clara's heart broke for Louise. Even at peace time the world was still such a harsh and unfair place.

"I'm fine, thank you," Louise said but even from a distance Clara could easily tell she struggled to swallow down her tears.

"I do hope he didn't suffer. He was such a good man."

"He was, thank you. And from what I've been told he didn't. He was killed during an attempt to escape so his last thoughts would have been of trying to get home to us."

"Let us be grateful for that. And at least you have little Anna to help you through it. Children give you so much strength in these tough days, don't they?"

"They do. I don't know what I'd do without her."

Louise walked further down the road but Clara didn't follow. She took one last look at Camille and waved. Then she turned around and left in the opposite direction without looking back. Just as she turned the corner, she thought she heard Camille say "Mama" again. But she forced herself to keep walking.

***

"I couldn't take her." Clara said as she fell into Daniel's arms. "Our darling girl, I couldn't take her." Daniel stroked her hair as she cried into his shoulder.

He waited for her to calm down before asking what had happened.

"She lost everything, Daniel. She saved me and Camille and she lost everything." Clara told him about the conversation she overheard.

"Both her parents died during the war, she lost her sweet Anna and now Peter will never return to her. Camille is all she has left. How could I take her away from her after all she risked for us?" Daniel wiped away her tears.

"Did she see you?" He asked after a while.

"No. She thinks we didn't survive. Was I wrong to leave her?"

"No," he whispered. "You've paid your debt now. She's in good hands, my love. We can let her go." Clara cried quietly on Daniel's shoulder. Tears of sadness for the loss of her baby mixed with ones of happiness because all three of them survived. She knew Camille and Louise would live a happy life together and that was all that mattered. It was good.

Chapter Forty-Six

Amsterdam, January 2001

The hospital room was surprisingly comfortable. Clara's bed was next to the window looking out over the city. She was barely visible with her pallor almost matching the white sheets. Sophia wiped the tears from her face and took Clara's frail hand in hers.

"Don't cry, little one," she said with a voice that sounded as brittle as dried autumn leaves. "I'll finally be able to rest. Life has made me very tired."

"I'll miss you."

"Not as much as I'll miss you. Soon I'll be with your mama and papa and we'll all look out for you."

Clara's eyes slowly closed. The pain meds were making her drowsy and she often dozed off for a few minutes. Sophia stroked her hand and waited for her to wake up.

"Can I ask you a question about the war? Or really about after it ended," Sophia asked when Clara had woken up.

"Sure, it's a long time ago but I'll try to remember." Sophia smiled, she knew that her grandmother remembered every single thing about that time but the temptation to pretend to have forgotten, so she didn't have to relive it, sometimes got the better of her.

"Why did you never get back in touch with Louise? I'm sure she would have loved to know you'd survived when she thought you hadn't."

"I nearly did, many times. When you share such a time together as we did, the connection you feel with someone is incredibly strong. I'd have loved to be friends after it all ended but what would have happened to Camille? I couldn't take her back but I also couldn't let Louise live with the guilt knowing she's got my baby. It was better for everyone to leave things as they were."

"But, didn't you miss Camille?"

"My heart aches for my little girl every single day and I'd have given anything to see her again. Anything, apart from the risk to ruin her happiness. Even when she was a grown woman herself, what if she didn't know what HAD happened? What if, to protect her, Louise never told her? I'd come in and turn her whole world upside down for selfish reasons only. No, I decided that if they're happy, leave them be. If they're not, they'll come looking." Clara's eyes were filled with tears, yet still she smiled at Sophia.

"All those years ago, I decided to leave my baby with Louise. It was the right decision, I still believe it is, and I'll stick to it until the day I die."

Chapter Forty-Seven

"Can you believe all along it was my mum I was looking for."

"It's quite the story!" Jack said.

For a while they talked about their childhoods, jobs, hobbies, Sarah's plans for the future, of which she had none and eventually religion. When the thought hit Sarah, she wondered if Sophia had been gently steering the conversation in this direction on purpose.

"So my mum was Jewish?" Sarah asked. Judging by the look on Jack's face she wasn't the only one who hadn't thought of it before.

"Yes, she was. And so are you, Sarah."

"What do you mean?"

"You're a Jew," Sophia said.

"But I'm an atheist, always have been."

"The things is when it comes to being Jewish, it doesn't really matter what you believe or what you practise. You were born to a Jewish mother which means you will always be a Jew and so will your children."

Sarah was struggling to process all the information that just seemed to keep coming, not in the least the realisation that Emma had been Jewish.

"Do you think my mum knew?" Sarah asked Sophia as they were getting ready to leave.

"I don't know. But it makes sense to assume that, as she left the diary out for you to find, she did. I think either she knew the full story and she wanted you to know as well or she didn't but thought you might want to just know a bit more about your nanna's and your mum's past. Either way, she probably thought it would help you deal with losing her." Sarah would never find out what her mum did or didn't know but it really didn't matter. Whatever reason she had for not telling her the truth in the past or for leaving the diary out, Sarah knew that she'd have done what she thought was best for Sarah. And that was all she needed to know. She gave Sophia a hug and thanked her for everything.

"Will you come see me again?" Sophia asked as she held Sarah's hands. Looking into Sophia's eyes, which were so similar to hers, Sarah felt connected to her in a way only family can and she could tell Sophia felt the same.

"Most definitely. I don't have any plans to go back to England any time soon, especially not now I've found you." Both women smiled through the tears which had managed to escape. There was no need to explain how they felt as they knew they both felt exactly the same. No longer alone in the world. No longer on their own.

"What's wrong?" Sarah asked noticing Jack's quietness.

"Are you really not going back to England?"

When Sarah had told Sophia she had no plans to go back, she hadn't considered what that meant for her and Jack.

"I don't know. I never came to Amsterdam with the intention of staying but my marriage is over, we're selling the house, what do I have to go back for?"

Jack looked into her eyes and then looked away.

Old Sarah would have moved back to England with him in a heartbeat. New Sarah, though, realised it was important to be where she felt she belonged.

"You can always move to Amsterdam," Sarah suggested only half joking.

"Okay," Jack said and he kissed her hard on the lips. She gently pushed him away and looked at him with cocked eyebrows.

"What do you mean okay?"

"Okay, I'll move to Amsterdam."

"Just like that?"

"Yeah, just like that. I've been thinking a lot about what I want in life and the only thing I'm sure of is that I want to spend more time with you. So if you feel the same and you're not coming back to England, I'll move here."

Jack looked more like he'd just decided what flavour ice cream he fancied rather than in which country he would live, and Sarah loved him for it.

"Are you sure?"

"I've never been more sure of anything in my entire life, Sarah. I know we've only known each other for a short while but you told me yourself I had to stop putting my life on hold for others. Well, this is me moving on. This is me doing what I want for a change. And I want you."

"I want you too."

Jack held her so tight Sarah knew that he'd never let her go.

Chapter Forty-Eight

As soon as the lights went out, the audience disappeared. Behind the conductor there was only black. The cellos started and soon it'd be Sarah's turn. She felt the other second violins get ready. Two more beats, one, and they were off. The violas joined with their warm tones and the first violins completed the group. The music pulsed through Sarah's body and she barely looked at her sheets. There was no need. She knew where she was going and the melody guided her along the way.

***

When she'd performed this piece with the orchestra in England, she'd been pregnant with Emma and it had been an exhausting performance. The last one before she went off on maternity leave, but also the best performance Sarah had ever been part of. It was one of those rare evenings where everyone was completely in tune with each other and the orchestra was like a magical creature moving through the music. It had been the perfect last night at work and even though Sarah was more than ready for a break, she also couldn't wait to come back to this after spending a few months with the baby.

***

All day Sarah had been anxious about the evening's performance. She knew, technically, she was more than capable. Even after she quit the orchestra and took to full time teaching, she still practised a couple of hours each day. Almost as if she'd always known this chapter of her life hadn't completely finished yet. She knew the piece inside out but images of her last ever performance, after she'd returned following Emma's death, haunted her still. The shaky hands, the many mistakes, the pretending she was counting a break when really she'd lost track completely and was desperately searching her sheets for a point where she could re-join the rest of the violins. It had only taken 90 minutes for her career to be ruined.

It was one of her new students who'd told her about the opening for second violin in the semi-professional orchestra made up mostly of musicians who were unable to combine their family responsibilities with full-time performing. The monthly concerts were a perfect way to satisfy the yearning to play for an audience without the demanding routine of a professional orchestra.

Only the conductor was aware of her last disastrous performance. His confidence in Sarah had been steady and he'd refused her request to sit at the back.

"You're my best second violin, Sarah. If the section hadn't been full, you'd be a first. There's no way I'm letting you hide in the back. You're ready for this, all you have to do is embrace it and enjoy."

He'd been right, she was ready. As soon as she played her first note, her fear and doubts drowned in the waves of the music. She didn't notice the conductor checking to make sure she was okay, nor was she aware of the audience. During a two-bar rest, she adjusted her position slightly to allow some space for her growing tummy. It had been quite a shock for them finding out Sarah was pregnant so soon after they moved in together, but nothing had prepared them for seeing two heartbeats at the 12-week scan. They were both over the moon although Sarah couldn't help feeling anxious. How would she cope when they got ill? And would they look like Emma? She quickly rejoiced when they found out they were girls and decided they'd name them Clara and Louise.

When the applause roared through the concert hall, Sarah knew this wasn't just a fresh start, it was also closure. She caught Jack's eye in the audience and felt hope for a happy future. Emma wouldn't be replaced by the two little lives growing inside her, but they would give her the chance of being happy again. And a chance to finally let go.

Chapter Forty-Nine

Sarah struggled for a long while deciding what to do about Anna's grave in the back garden. In the end she decided she didn't want to disturb her peace. If her nanna would've wanted to move her, she'd had plenty of time to do it. The fact she didn't was reason enough for Sarah not to either. Anna would stay where she was. Instead Sarah commissioned an artist to create a wooden bench incorporating an A and an E to remember the two girls who died so young. When it was finished, Sarah, Jack and Sophia placed it over Anna's grave, underneath the olive tree, on a cold and bright March morning, just as the sun peeped over the fence.

Finding Sophia had made Sarah a whole new person. It had taken her a while to come to terms with the truth about her past, but in the end, knowing what happened and how both women dealt with it, made Sarah respect them even more. And even though she still found it hard to understand why her mum never told her, especially after her nanna passed away, at least she now knew. She missed her mum terribly but because of the diary she'd left for her, Sarah was no longer alone.

After placing the bench, Sarah and Sophia went to the cemetery to put flowers on three graves. First Clara's, who just so happened to be buried only two rows from Louise, who they visited next. Both Sarah and Sophia knew their grandmothers would be delighted to be so close together after almost a lifetime apart. Sarah's mum laid next to Louise. When she arranged her mum's funeral she found out that when her nanna died, her mum had bought the grave next to hers to make sure they'd never be separated. Not even by death. Louise and the girl who was left behind. Anna to some, but always Camille.

The End

Acknowledgements

It took me a long time to write this book and it would have taken even longer without the help of some amazing people.

My mum, who read everything three, four or even five times and spent hours researching with the help of Eva van Dijk from Amsterdam Odyssey.

The wonderful writers of Ipswich Writer's Group, who with their, sometimes brutal, feedback and relentless cliché policing (Paul!), helped shape the story to what it is today.

Franzi, whose feedback fixed the main character and who also designed the beautiful cover.

Ines, my wonderful editor, whose feedback was truly invaluable.

Glen, for saving me from a title disaster.

My dad and sister for their unwavering support and words of encouragement.

All my friends and family who either read it and gave feedback or showed their support in other ways.

Jade, for always being there.

Erin, the best friend one can wish for, who read the book several times and spent hours listening to me going on about it.

And last but not least, my grandmother and all the other brave women who, during WWII, risked their own lives to save others. This is for you!

A note from Elske

Thank you so much for choosing to read Left Behind, it really means the world to me.

If you enjoyed reading it, please leave a review if you'd like to, or let me know via my website, www.elskehoweler.com, I'd love to hear what you think.

Lots of love
Elske Höweler
Suffolk, 2020

Printed in Great Britain
by Amazon